All Your Loving

BACHELORS & BRIDESMAIDS (#3)

BARBARA FREETHY

All Your Loving

This is a work of fiction. Names, characters, places, and incidents are products of the author's imagination or are used fictitiously. Any resemblance to actual events, locales, organizations or persons, living or dead, is entirely coincidental.

For information contact: barbara@barbarafreethy.com

Chapter One

"I need a man," Melanie Hall announced, opening the door to Julie Michaels' office late Tuesday afternoon. "Handsome, rich, talented and famous, and you're going to get him for me."

Julie smiled. "Sure I am. Right after I find one for myself." She pushed a stack of brochures and envelopes across her small, cluttered desk. "Why don't you make yourself useful and help me stuff some envelopes?"

Melanie pushed the offending pile away. "We can do those later. Right now we have a bigger problem."

"Finding you a man?"

"Not me, the Foundation. Kevin Markham just dropped out of the Celebrity Cook-Off."

"No," she said in disappointed surprise. Kevin Markham, an A-List actor was their big draw for the upcoming fundraiser and to lose him now was a huge blow. "What happened?"

"He got a DUI last night and has already gone into rehab. His publicist just called me. He won't be available for our events or any appearances for at least a month."

"Damn. That's bad news."

"It is." Melanie sat down in the chair in front of Julie's desk. "I've been racking my brain for a replacement. We need someone with wow factor—a bigger than life hero, who will help us sell out the rest of the event and do some press for us."

By the gleam in Melanie's eyes, Julie could tell she had someone in mind. "Who are you talking about?"

"Matt Kingsley."

Her stomach knotted at the mention of the star hitter for the San Francisco Cougars.

"Any chance you could get to him?"

"No," she said immediately.

"You don’t have any connections from when your dad was playing?"

She shook her head, her stomach tightening at the mention of her father. "My dad left me with nothing and that includes connections."

"We're desperate," Melanie said quietly. "You know how important this fundraiser is for the Foundation. It's the backbone of our budget, and expenses have been much higher than we expected this year. If we don't pull in a significant amount of funds at the cook-off, we may have to shut down some of our programs. We have to replace Markham with someone big."

Julie leaned back against her chair with a sigh. Melanie's words were not news. She was very aware of the shoestring nature of their budget. "But why Matt Kingsley?"

"Because we've already asked everyone else we know," Melanie said practically. "Unless your friend Michael Stafford can come up with anymore football players to help out."

"I already signed up three of his friends for the telethon next month. I can't tap that well again so soon."

"Exactly. That's why we need Matt Kingsley. He hit over .500 in the playoffs last year and practically won the division title single-handedly. He's a legend in the making.

He's also sexy as hell. The press loves him. The fans love him. Heck, I even love him. And I'm sure you would, too, if you didn't have a hang-up about baseball players."

Julie stood up, walked over to the window and gazed blankly out at the colorful crowds strolling along Fisherman's Wharf. She had had enough of baseball legends to last a lifetime. Her father, Jack Michaels, had been one of the greatest pitchers in the National League. But as a man, a father and a husband, he had not come close to being a hero.

She turned back to face Melanie. "If you want Kingsley, go for it. You don't need me."

"I do need you. I've called his agent numerous times with no response, and I can't get past the reception in the Cougars' front office. I need you to work your magic, Julie. You're the best at signing reluctant celebrities."

She was pretty good at wrangling volunteers, but not when it came to baseball players. She hadn't been to a baseball stadium since her father had destroyed her family.

"I told you, I don't have any connections," she said.

"You have your last name," Robert Hudson interjected.

Julie looked up as the executive director entered her office. Robert was her boss and a friend, but he could also be ruthless when it came to the Foundation. He had started the organization with his brother who had lost a child to cancer. For Robert, their work wasn't just charity, it was personal.

"My last name isn't going to matter to the Cougars," she protested, even though she knew deep down she probably did have a better chance of getting to Matt Kingsley because of her last name. Dale Howard, one of her father's best friends, was still the general manager of the Cougars. But she didn't want to talk to Dale anymore than she wanted to talk to anyone else on the team.

Robert gave her a steely look that told her he didn't think much of her defense. "We need you, Julie. This is for the kids."

"You don't have to remind me," she said with a sigh.

"Then put your personal feelings aside and get us Matt Kingsley," he said.

If it wasn't for the kids, she wouldn't even consider what they were asking, but both Robert and Melanie were right. They needed a superstar to replace Markham and sell out the event, and if Matt Kingsley participated, it would probably be standing room only.

"Okay," she said with a sigh. "I'll give it a shot. But I'd have a backup plan ready to go in case I strike out."

Melanie smiled. "See, you're already thinking in baseball terms."

"But don't think about striking out," Robert told her. "We need a home run."

* * *

Two days later Julie drove into the San Francisco stadium parking lot determined to make good on her promise to Melanie and Robert. She'd called Matt Kingsley's agent a dozen times with no return call. She'd also checked in with the Cougars' front office and had been just as stymied. She'd even tried to reach her father's old friend Dale Howard, but he was out of town. She was out of options and quickly running out of time. She needed to get to the man himself, so she was going to do what she'd never in a million years thought she'd do—she was going to stalk a baseball player.

Spring training would be starting in three weeks, but until then, the Cougars were holding informal light practices for the players who lived in the Bay Area, and she'd seen on a recent sports report that Kingsley was still in town. The timing was actually good. If Matt was in town now, there was no reason that he wouldn't be here a week from Saturday when the cook-off was to be held. He shouldn't have to leave for Arizona until a week after that.

A car horn blared in her ear, and she instinctively hit the brakes as a carload of three teenage girls hurtled past her. Apparently, she wasn't the only one trying to catch up with a ballplayer today.

After parking the car, she walked through the lot, seeing the massive stadium rising up in front of her. The queasiness in her stomach grew as memories flooded her mind. The stands were empty, but in her mind she could hear the cheers and applause of game day. She could smell the hot dogs and onions and feel the damp windiness of the walkways. As a kid, she'd spent a lot of days and nights at ballparks around the country, and she could still remember the long cold nights when the game went into extra innings or the stunningly hot doubleheaders on the weekends. She'd filled herself with hot dogs and peanuts and kept track of every play so she could talk to her dad about the game later. Not that they'd actually talked much, but in her head she'd always hoped they would, and she'd always wanted to be ready, to prove she was *his girl*. Unfortunately, whatever happy memories she'd had of those days had been ripped out of her head by all the pain and anger that followed her father's betrayal.

When she saw the crowd of adoring women waiting in front of the players' entrance, she wanted to flee. It was so familiar it was frightening. She could see herself as a young girl following proudly behind her dad as he made his way through the crush of fans.

He had been her hero then. He used to put her on his shoulders so she could see among the throng of people. She'd felt so special, so important…

She forced the old images out of her head and paused at the edge of the crowd. She hadn't expected to find so many girls waiting, but she should have. The Cougars had been in the World Series last year. They had a lot of fans. She tried to squeeze past some teens in front of her, but was unsuccessful.

"Hey, wait your turn," a young girl snapped. She then pushed her aside, driving an elbow into her rib cage, and as Julie winced in pain, two more girls pushed their way past her. She was buried in the middle of the crowd.

She had to stand on tiptoe to see over the people in front of her, and she began to realize the foolishness of her mission. Matt Kingsley wasn't going to stop and chat with her, not with this mass of women waiting outside the entrance. She needed to find another way.

She was just turning to leave when the door opened and two young men walked out.

The freshness of their smiles as they looked at the women was enough to tell her that neither was the infamous Matt Kingsley. They were too caught up in the excitement to be the veteran ace hitter for the ball club.

They stopped to sign a few autographs, reveling in the attention. One of the young girls went so far as to climb over the barricade in an attempt to steal a kiss. A guard immediately came to the player's aid, but no one seemed to be in a hurry to break the embrace.

Julie turned away with a sigh. This approach was definitely not going to work. She had seen her father dodge enough wild fans to know that Matt Kingsley wasn't going to just waltz through this pack of wolves.

She walked slowly back toward the parking lot. It was then that she spotted a very tall, well-built man striding toward a bright red Ferrari parked well away from the other cars. She knew instantly that she had found her man. Everything about him—from the stylishly cut brown hair, to the tan, to the tight jeans—spelled superstar.

In that split second, she didn't stop to think about his reaction, she just plunged forward, anxious to get the job done before she lost her nerve. She reached him just as he got to the door of his car. Breathlessly, she grabbed his arm. "Mr. Kingsley. Wait, please. I need to talk to you."

He looked down at her in surprise. "What?" he demanded.

She looked into his light green eyes and felt the breath catch in her throat. No wonder the man was a star. He was gorgeous.

"Do you want an autograph?" he asked briskly, removing her hand from his arm.

"No. I want you," she mumbled, saying the first thing that came into her mind as she stared into his incredibly sexy eyes.

"Sorry, I'm not available. Why don't you try one of the guys over there?" He pointed to the group of players now talking to the crowd.

"No, wait. I don't mean you, exactly. I just want to talk to you. I have to ask you something—"

"Not today, sweetheart. I don't have time." His voice was filled with polite weariness.

"My name is Julie."

"Look, honey, I don't care what your name is. In fact, I think it's better if I don't know. Please just go away. I'm tired. I want to go home and go to bed. Alone."

"I just want to talk to you for a minute," she said in exasperation.

"Talk? That's a new one."

"Mr. Kingsley—"

"If I give you what you want, will you leave?"

"Yes, of course," she snapped, unaware of his intentions, until he put his arms around her. "What—what do you think you're doing?"

"Giving you what you want," he growled into her ear as his lips covered hers in a long, hot kiss.

She was so shocked by the onslaught, it took her a minute to react, and another minute to pull herself away from what was quite possibly the hottest kiss she'd ever had. "Stop," she said. "That's not what I want."

He looked at her in surprise, and then his eyes traveled down her body, taking in her business skirt and cream-colored blouse. His hands fell from her shoulders as he gave her a wary look. "Okay."

"That's it? Okay? You kiss me and then say okay?"

"What do you want me to say? You told me you wanted me."

"Not like that."

"I guess we got our signals crossed. I thought you were a fan. But come to think of it, you don't look like a groupie, you don't talk like one and you certainly don't kiss like one."

Julie's mouth dropped open at his provocative statement. "What do you mean, I don't kiss like a groupie?" She mentally kicked herself for asking such a leading question. What difference did it make what he thought of the way she kissed? "Forget I asked that."

He shrugged. "Fine. So, who are you and what do you want?"

She stared at him blankly, finally realizing that she was going to be given an opportunity to explain. She took a deep breath, taking a minute to regain her poise. "My name is Julie Michaels. I work for the California Children's Foundation. I came to see you, hoping I could persuade you to participate in our fundraiser next week. I know you're busy, but it's for a really good cause."

"They all are. I wish I could help you, but right now I need to concentrate one hundred percent on baseball. Another time, perhaps, but not now."

"It's only one night, a couple of hours. And it would mean so much." She hated herself for having to beg, but it was important that he realize what was at stake. "The kids, they—"

"I said no," he snapped. "There are a lot of charities who want my help. I can't participate in everything. I'm sorry."

She shouldn't have been surprised at his attitude. Her father had never gone out of his way to help anyone. It was always about baseball; that was the only thing that mattered to him. And Matt Kingsley was just like her dad.

"You're sorry?" She shook her head, the words pouring out of her before she could stop herself. "I don't think so. You're so caught up in your own star-studded world that you can't think about anybody beside yourself. You're worrying about hitting a ball over a fence, and we're trying to help children survive cancer and child abuse. God, I hate macho baseball players," she said passionately, her voice ringing through the parking lot.

Matt's jaw dropped in surprise.

"Look, there he is," a young girl shouted from the distant crowd as their argument drew attention.

Julie whirled around as the crowd turned toward them, their adoring faces filled with excitement. Matt Kingsley was their hero, a man who rose above all others, but she couldn't see what they saw, or maybe she just didn't want to.

As the girls ran toward them, she turned and walked away. Matt might have turned her down, but at least she'd put him in the middle of a pack of hungry teenage wolves. It wasn't much, but it was something.

* * *

The drive from the baseball stadium in China Basin to the Foundation offices near Fisherman's Wharf gave Julie time to think, and her anger was slowly replaced by guilt and embarrassment. She had never spoken like that to anyone, especially a potential celebrity participant. But Matt Kingsley's curt refusal had opened up her old wounds. She banged the steering wheel in frustration. When was she going to be free of the anger and pain that came with memories of her father?

It had been ten years since she had seen her dad and ten years since she had attended a baseball game, but the mere mention of the sport had sent her emotions spinning out of control. Within minutes of arriving at the stadium, she'd changed from a calm, poised businesswoman into a crazy person.

Her guilt deepened as she walked into the office and saw Robert and Melanie working together in the conference room. The three of them were a team, and they had raised a lot of money for the children they served. She didn't want to let them down, but they were going to have to find someone else to star in the cook-off.

They looked up expectantly as she pushed open the door.

"I'm sorry," she said.

Melanie frowned. "You didn't see him?"

"Damn." Robert shook his head in frustration. "We need that man. We'll have to try something else. I found out last night that he goes to the Royal Athletic Club every morning between six and eight o'clock. That might be a good spot to get to him."

"I don't think so," Julie replied.

Robert looked at her in surprise. "You're not giving up, are you? This is too important to quit on, Julie."

"I did see Matt Kingsley." She took a deep breath. "I spoke to him. He said no, and then—then I insulted him."

"You didn't," Melanie breathed.

"I'm afraid so."

"What exactly do you mean—you insulted him?" Robert asked.

"I asked him to participate in the fundraiser, and he said no. Then I got angry. He wouldn't even give me a chance to explain, to tell him what we're all about."

Melanie looked at her in amazement. "What did you say? I don't know how you had the nerve to insult someone like that."

"He's just a man, and not a very nice one. I'm sorry that I let you guys down. But I honestly don't think there's anything I could have said that would have made him participate. His mind was made up before I ever opened my mouth. I didn't insult him until after he said no."

The receptionist buzzed the phone to tell Robert that one of the board members was on the phone.

He sighed when he heard the name. "The last thing I want to do is tell Emily Davenport that we failed on getting Matt Kingsley. Her husband is a season ticket holder and one of their biggest fans."

"Maybe we can get some of the other Cougars," Melanie suggested.

"Matt Kingsley is the Cougars. The rest of the guys look like amateurs next to him." Robert got to his feet. "I'm not giving up on Kingsley yet. There must be a way to change his mind. Think about it."

Julie nodded, even though she knew that she could think about it forever, and there was nothing she could do to change things. She sat down as Robert left the room. "I really blew this one, Mel. I should have handled his refusal better, tried to charm him into finding out more about us."

"Well, at least you actually spoke to him. That's better than Robert or I did. What did he look like, anyway? Was he as sexy and attractive as his posters?"

"He was," she admitted. "I just wish he had more compassion, more sensitivity to go with that face and body." Her voice hardened. "But the man has only one thing on his mind and that's baseball."

"Maybe that's why he's the best."

"I suppose. I'll call the Cougars again and see if any other players are available. But I think we need to come up with some other ideas." She made her way back to her office and dove into work. It focused her brain on what was important and kept the emotions at bay.

She worked into the evening, barely noticing when Melanie stopped in to say goodbye. It was only when a knock came at her door that she realized the office had grown dark. She switched on her desk lamp, the light outlining a shadowy figure behind the glass panel. She was completely alone in the office. Her nerves tingled as the knock came again, and then the door slowly opened.

Chapter Two

"Julie Michaels." Matt Kingsley said her name with satisfaction, savoring her look of surprise. It had taken him some effort to track her down, time he really didn't have to waste, but after their encounter at the ballpark, he hadn't been able to put her out of his mind.

She was prettier than he remembered, her eyes a beautiful sky blue framed by dark lashes, her blonde hair swirling around her shoulders in silky waves, her form fitting skirt and silky top clinging to some very nice curves. She was definitely not a groupie.

Julie rose to her feet, her eyes wary. "What are you doing here?"

"Looking for you." He walked into the room and moved a stack of folders off the chair in front of her desk. "Do you mind?"

She shook her head. "No, please sit down."

"It took me a while to find you," he said as she sat down behind her desk. "I couldn't remember the name of your organization, but when I asked at the Cougars' front office if they knew anything about you, they gave me this address."

"I—I honestly don't know what to say. I thought you'd made your decision clear earlier."

"I thought so, too. But then I had second thoughts." He

glanced around her tiny office. It was typical of a small nonprofit organization. There were stacks of banners and posters in one corner, a desk overflowing with paperwork, and T-shirts for an upcoming walkathon piled on top of a filing cabinet. "Looks like you have a lot of events going on."

"Always. It's how we raise money." She paused. "Why are you here?" she asked, fiddling with her ballpoint pen.

As he gazed at her, he felt a little entranced by the way her golden hair caught the light from her desk lamp, almost like a halo for an angel—a wary, pissed off angel.

He leaned forward and picked up one of the photographs on her desk. It was a photo of a group of young teenagers in matching California Children's Foundation shirts. "Who are these kids?"

"They're a mix of kids who have been homeless, are in foster care, or are being raised by single parents with very low income. Their circumstances are helped by the services at Baycrest House, which the Foundation supports. They have after school programs, tutoring, meals, showers, places to sleep, and although they try to help the whole family, their focus is on the children who may slip through the cracks. Those particular kids are doing really well in school now, and they've become mentors for the younger children. They also do volunteer jobs here at the Foundation. They're really great."

Her voice warmed and her eyes softened as she spoke of the kids, and he was beginning to see just how passionate she was about her job and also how personal her job was to her. She wasn't just about raising money and asking for things; she really cared. And it had been a while since he'd met anyone who cared about the bigger picture of the world. He liked that. He also felt even guiltier now for how he'd shut her down earlier.

"I can give you a brochure on that program and others that we fund," Julie said. "If you're interested."

"Sure," he said. "But I doubt the brochure will bring the program alive the way you just did."

"I wrote most of it, so hopefully it will." She paused, her lips tightening as she drew in a breath. "You said you had second thoughts. What does that mean?"

"I want to apologize."

Her eyebrows shot up in amazement. "Seriously?"

"Yes. We got our signals crossed earlier. I've been swamped with business demands the last few days and trips back and forth across the country. I got off a plane this morning at eleven and had a poor batting practice right before I talked to you. When you caught up with me, I wasn't in the best mood. It's not an excuse, but I hope it gives my actions some context."

"It does," she said slowly. "And I really appreciate you taking the time to apologize. I'm sorry, too, for what I said. I had no right to yell at you because you said no. You certainly don't have to participate in our event. I know you must have a lot of demands on your time."

"I do. So tell me about this event you want me to participate in."

"It's a celebrity cook-off that will be used specifically to provide another year of funding for Baycrest House as well as two other afterschool programs for kids in need. If we somehow manage to go over our target goal, we're also hoping to buy some new medical equipment for a pediatric urgent care center that was recently set up in the Tenderloin to serve kids who don't have good access to healthcare."

"All right, I'm sold," he said lightly.

"Really? Does that mean you're going to help us out?"

He nodded. "What do I need to do?"

"We'd like you to be a chef in our Celebrity Cook-Off a

week from Saturday at the Ambassador Hotel. We'll have a dozen celebrities cooking and then putting their dishes in front of a panel of celebrity judges, but you would be the star. It's not a huge commitment of time."

"I'll do it," he said. "But I want to know something first."

"What's that?"

"When we met earlier, when I said no, you said you hated baseball players, hated people like me."

She paled at his words. "I shouldn't have said that. I'm sorry."

"That's an apology, not an explanation."

"I was just overstating an opinion."

"What happened? Did some baseball player screw you over?"

She hesitated, as if debating whether she wanted to answer his question. "You could say that, yes."

"We're not all the same, you know."

"I haven't seen much evidence to support that opinion."

"Who was the player? Is he still in the game?"

"Why don't we talk more about the cook-off?"

"We'll get to the details. You tarred me with the brush of some other guy, and I want to know who it was."

Her jaw tightened. "You heard my last name, right?"

Her question set him back, and he had to think for a moment. "Michaels?"

"Ring a bell?"

Their gazes met, clung together.

Anger burned in her eyes along with what looked like pain.

"Are you talking about Jack Michaels?" he asked slowly.

"Yes. Jack is my father."

He felt like she'd punched him in the stomach. "You're

Jack Michaels' kid?"

"I guess you know him then."

"I do—really well. Jack was a mentor to me when I first came up from the minors. It was his last season in the league. He was forty-one years old, and he pitched a no-hitter in the playoffs. It was one of the most amazing feats I'd ever seen." He shook his head, thinking back to that day ten years ago. He'd been a nineteen-year-old rookie and Jack had seemed like a God to him, to everyone on the team. "Did you see that game?"

"No, my father had left my mother and me that year, so we weren't going to his games. I'm sure his twenty-two-year-old girlfriend was in the stands."

Now he knew where the anger and pain came from. "I'm sorry. I guess I knew Jack was divorced, but I didn't know the circumstances."

She shrugged. "It doesn't matter. Let's talk about the cook-off."

"All right. There is one small problem."

"What's that?"

"I don't know how to cook."

A frown drew her brows together. "You must know how to cook something—spaghetti, chicken, steak?"

"No, no and no."

She gave him a disbelieving look. "Are you sure you're not just looking for another way out?"

"I came all the way over here to find you. Would I really be looking for an escape route now?" Actually, he should be looking for an escape route, because the beautiful Julie with her golden hair, blue eyes, sexy curves and deeply ingrained hatred of ballplayers was presenting an intriguing challenge, a challenge he really should stay the hell away from, especially now that he knew she was Jack Michaels' daughter.

"You tell me," she returned.

"I'm in, but I can't cook, so is there something else I could do?"

"No, each celebrity will cook their meal in a unique kitchen area, specifically designed for that celebrity by volunteer interior designers. If you're going to participate, they'll create a kitchen for you with probably a baseball theme or you can certainly have input if you like, but we're running a little short on time."

"Why is that?" he asked curiously. "I usually get invitations months in advance. Someone dropped out, didn't they?"

"Yes," she admitted. "Otherwise, we do prefer to give as much notice as possible."

"So I'm your second choice."

"You're a star, Mr. Kingsley. You would always be everyone's first choice, but you're not easy to get to. Other celebrities like these opportunities to create an aura of generosity."

He liked her candid response. One thing about Julie Michaels—she was not a bull-shitter.

"We were working with Kevin Markham," she continued. "I don't know if you're familiar with him."

"Action hero? Yeah, I know his work."

"He just went into rehab, so we need to replace him."

"Okay, then I can only see one solution to the problem. You'll have to teach me how to cook in the next ten days."

She immediately shook her head. "I don't think so."

"You don't know how to cook?"

"I do, but I can't teach you."

"Why not?"

"Because I have a job that takes up all my days and quite frankly a lot of my nights, especially before big events."

"I'm busy, too. We're talking about one meal. If you

can't teach me something I can make, then I can't participate. I'm not going to embarrass myself."

"I'm sure you could hire a chef to give you a lesson."

He could hire a chef, and that would probably be a smarter move, but right now all he could think about was locking down a date with Julie Michaels, and he knew she wasn't going to willingly spend time with him unless she was getting something out of it.

"I'm not interested in hiring someone. That's going to take effort and time. So here's the deal—you give me one cooking lesson, and I'm yours for the cook-off. What do you say?"

She had no choice, and they both knew it.

"Fine," she said with a sigh. "What night?"

"How about tomorrow? Friday night? Or do you have a date?" It occurred to him that he didn't even know if Julie was single, although there was no ring on her finger.

"I can make tomorrow," she said slowly.

"Great. What are we going to make?"

"I won't make anything—you will. I'm just going to be advising." Julie paused. "What do you like to eat?"

"Anything and everything. I'm not picky."

"I'll look through some recipes and pick something that isn't too hard and that will be easy for the hotel kitchen to recreate for all the guests. While your entry will go to the panel of judges, everyone in the room will be tasting the same dishes prepared by the hotel chefs. We'll need to change the recipe to give it a more personal Matt Kingsley spin, but that should work. Do you like hot and spicy?"

He smiled at the question. "Hot, sweet, spicy, sexy…it's all good."

Her cheeks warmed at his words. "You're a troublemaker, aren't you?"

"I've been called worse. Give me your number, and I'll

text you my address. If I'm going to learn to cook, it might as well be in my own kitchen."

"Where do you live?"

"I have a condo near the ballpark at Brandon and Second."

She nodded. "There's a supermarket not far from there. I'll meet you there at six-thirty tomorrow night, and we can buy the ingredients together."

"Shopping and cooking?" he asked doubtfully, suddenly wondering what he'd gotten himself into.

"They do go together," she said with a smile as she got to her feet. "You're quite spoiled, aren't you?"

He stood up. "It's been a good decade," he admitted. "But my mother would be horrified to think I was spoiled."

"Really? Even though she never taught you how to cook?"

"She worked two jobs when I was growing up. She didn't have time to cook or to teach me how to do it," he said, remembering the long days when he'd waited for her to come home, only to have to see her rush out the door again for a second job late in the night. He'd made a promise to himself when he was very young that someday he would find a way to make sure she didn't have to work that hard.

"Sorry," Julie said, guilt in her eyes. "I seem to be really judgmental when it comes to you."

"To me? Or to everyone?" he couldn't help asking.

"You seem to have brought out the worst in me, but it's not really you, it's what you do for a living. However, I do want to thank you for agreeing to participate in the cook-off. Your support at this event will make a huge difference. Let me show you out."

She walked him down the hall, past the darkened conference room and empty cubicles.

"You're closing down this place," he commented.

"I have a few things to finish up. When you work for a non-profit, you do what has to be done, no matter how long it takes."

"I can see that you're a hard worker."

"I don't know any other way to work," she replied.

He smiled. "You might be surprised to know it's exactly the same for me." He paused at the door. "Goodnight Julie Michaels. See you tomorrow."

"Tomorrow," she muttered, then shut the door behind him.

* * *

Julie leaned against the door and let out a breath. She still couldn't quite believe Matt Kingsley had tracked her down, that he'd agreed to participate in the cook-off, and most importantly that she'd somehow been talked into giving him a cooking lesson at his home. What a crazy turn of events. She hadn't thought she'd ever see him again after the way things had ended in the parking lot, but Matt had surprised her with an apology.

She almost wished he hadn't come to find her, because seeing him tonight had sent some ridiculous nervous shivers down her spine, and while he'd been talking to her, she'd found herself thinking about his mouth, his lips, and the way his tongue had slid against the seam of her lips during their unexpected kiss.

He was a ballplayer, and she hated ballplayers, she reminded herself.

But Matt was turning out to be not that easy to hate. He was charming her, and she was letting his good looks and sexy smile get to her. That was just part of the game, she told herself. Of course, he knew how to get a woman to like him. Charm was part of the celebrity sports star package. But she knew what happened after all that. She'd seen her mother go through it, and the last thing she needed to do was follow her mother down that same path.

So she'd give Matt a cooking lesson and that would be that. He'd honor his commitment, and in a few weeks, she'd never have to see him again.

She made her way back to her office and had barely sat back down at her desk when her phone buzzed. Despite her very recent mental pep talk, her stomach turned over at the sight of Matt's name in her text messages.

"Looking forward to tomorrow," he said, his address following the brief message.

Yeah, he was definitely working the attentive angle. She leaned back in her chair with a sigh, feeling way too distracted and restless to keep working.

Picking up her phone again, she texted her friend Liz to see if she wanted to grab dinner. Liz sent back an immediate yes. She was looking at wedding venues with Kate so they'd both meet her in thirty minutes.

She sighed again. Liz's words reminded her that Liz was her third friend to get engaged in the last year, and soon she would be adding another bridesmaid's dress to her closet. Liz hadn't set a date for her wedding yet, but Julie had a feeling it would be soon. Liz's father was sick, and while he was holding his own at the moment, Liz very much wanted her dad to walk her down the aisle, so she would not go for a long engagement. Hopefully, her dad's health would remain stable and he would be by Liz's side on her wedding day. Liz's relationship with her father had always been so close, and Julie had sometimes been a little jealous of that.

She would have loved to have her father in her life. But even before the divorce, he'd rarely been around and afterward he'd disappeared. He'd moved on, and she doubted he'd ever looked back. Her father surrounded himself with people who adored him—people like Matt Kingsley. She'd seen Matt's face when she mentioned her father was the infamous Jack Michaels, and Matt had sat up a little straighter, obviously impressed. And it wasn't just that Matt knew of Jack but they'd played together. Jack had been Matt's mentor, so of course, Matt idolized her father. Jack Michaels was everyone's hero—but hers.

She needed to get Matt out of her life as fast as possible, because he was already bringing up way too many memories. Ten days, she told herself. Ten days and then she would never have to see him again. But she had a feeling those ten days were going to prove to be more than a little interesting and challenging.

Chapter Three

Liz Palmer was a brown-eyed blonde who'd been friends with Julie since middle school and Kate Marlowe was a pretty brunette Julie had met her first week in college. They'd been friends ever since. Liz worked in public relations and had just changed firms while Kate ran her own wedding planning business, which was actually picking up steam with so many of their friends getting married.

Drinks were followed by dinner at an Asian fusion restaurant in the Ferry Building where Julie listened to lots of wedding talk: cake-toppers, music, flowers, and invitations… the list seemed to go on and on. Thankfully, she didn't have to say much. Kate had a million ideas, and Liz was caught up in the giddy delight of being a bride. It was actually kind of funny to see Liz acting so dreamy. Until she'd fallen in love with Michael, Liz had been one of the more cynical members of their group of friends.

"Sorry," Liz said finally, giving her an apologetic smile. "I can't believe I've turned into one of those brides who talks only about her wedding."

"I can't either," Julie said dryly. "But don't apologize. I love seeing you happy and excited. I still haven't heard a wedding date though."

"That's dependent on the venue," Liz replied. "Kate

showed me a couple of places in the city today, but I think I want an outdoor wedding."

"I'm going to check with Maggie," Kate continued. "I want to see if we can possibly book the garden at the Stratton up in Napa."

Maggie was another one of their college friends. She was a desk clerk at a very upscale hotel in the wine country.

"That would be really nice," she said.

"But maybe too expensive unless Maggie can get us a deal," Liz said. "I'm also thinking about doing it down on the Peninsula, closer to my parents' house. The Delfina Inn on Skyline has a nice room and a beautiful view. It's kind of small, but it could work. And they said they might have a cancellation for June 20th."

"This June?" she asked in surprise. "That's only three months from now."

"Michael and I don't want a long engagement," Liz said. "Even though we only reconnected a few months ago, we feel like we've been in love since we were teenagers."

Julie nodded. She'd been around when the sparks had first flown between the teenaged Liz and Michael. "I get it. I think a June garden wedding would be perfect."

"We should know within the next few days about both places," Kate said. "Once we get the venue settled, everything else will fall into place." She smiled at Julie. "We'll have to start looking at bridesmaid's dresses again."

She groaned. "I'm beginning to think that pact we made at college graduation was a bad idea." Their group of eight girlfriends had made a vow that no matter how much time passed and how far they drifted apart, they would always be each other's bridesmaids.

"Actually, you won't need a bridesmaid's dress, Julie," Liz said, a sparkle in her brown eyes.

"Why not? Are you not having bridesmaids?" she asked

in surprise. "Or have you decided to drop me from the group?"

Liz made a face at her. "I'm having bridesmaids, but I want you to be my maid of honor, Julie. You and I go way back, and you've always been my best friend."

She felt a rush of emotion at Liz's words and her eyes blurred with unexpected tears. "I would love to be your maid of honor."

"Well, don't cry about it," Liz teased.

She gave her a smile. "I was just thinking about all those long talks we'd have late into the night about boys and our future. I'm so glad you're happy, and I can't wait to stand by your side. Thanks, Lizzie." She got up and gave Liz a hug. "I won't let you down."

"You never have," Liz returned, giving her a warm smile.

"So does Michael have his groomsmen lined up?" Julie asked as she sat back down.

"He's still figuring that out. He wasn't happy when I told him he needed seven guys to match my bridesmaids," Liz added with a laugh. "But I'm sure he can easily find that many men. He was on a football team after all."

She nodded. Michael Stafford had been a star quarterback up until a year ago when he'd blown out his knee and had to change his entire life around. "How's he doing in PR? Does he still have yearnings to go back to football?" she asked.

"As you know, he did some assistant coaching last season, and he's now getting offers from other teams to join their coaching staff on a permanent basis. I'm not sure what he's going to do. But whatever he decides, we'll make it work."

"What if that means moving somewhere else?" she asked.

Liz shrugged. "I love him. If he has to move, I'll move with him. And since we both work for Michael's sister, I'm pretty sure she'll allow us to work remotely. If that doesn't work, I'll figure something else out."

"You've always been so committed to having your own career," Julie said slowly, thinking how strange it was to hear Liz speak so cavalierly about her job. "Could you really just walk away from it so easily? Put it on the back burner so Michael can do what he wants?"

Liz smiled back at her with not a speck of doubt in her eyes. "I know it seems strange for me to say that I would give up everything I've worked to achieve for Michael, but the truth is that Michael is giving me the life and the love I've always wanted. I've realized since I met him that I was fighting a long time for the wrong thing, for someone else's dream and not mine. I'm going to work. I'll have my own career, and I will be damn good at it, but it's going to have to work with what Michael wants and needs, too. I really feel like we're partners now. We make compromises for each other."

"Do you think he'd make the same compromise for you?" she couldn't help asking.

"I'm sure he would," Liz said, giving her a speculative look. "Are we still talking about Michael?"

Liz had always been incredibly perceptive. "Maybe not," she admitted. "I don't have the best view of love, marriage and compromise, so just ignore me."

"You'll change your mind when you meet the right man," Kate interjected.

"You're such a romantic, Kate."

"Romance is my business."

Liz frowned, her gaze still on Julie. "What's going on with you? You've been a little moody since you got here?"

"I'm just tired."

"I don't think that's it, Jules. Come on, talk to us. We're your friends," Liz said.

She hesitated, then shrugged. "Fine, I've just been thinking a lot about my father today."

"Why? Did you hear from him?" Liz asked.

"No, but I had to go to the baseball park earlier today to try to sign Matt Kingsley up for the Celebrity Cook-Off, and the trip brought back a lot of memories."

"Is Matt going to participate?" Kate asked, an excited light in her eyes. "Because I'm definitely getting a ticket if he is. The guy is super hot and single."

"He is going to help us out. He wasn't going to at first, but somehow I convinced him."

"How did you do that?" Liz asked curiously.

She found herself giving them a helpless smile. "I kissed him."

"What?" Liz demanded, her question echoed immediately by Kate.

"We've been together for an hour," Kate said. "And you're just mentioning this now?"

"Well, he actually kissed me. He thought I was a groupie." She waved a hand in the air. "It was all a big misunderstanding. In the end, I got an apology and an agreement for him to participate in the fundraiser. So I guess it was worth it."

"How was the kiss?" Kate asked with interest.

She thought about the question for probably longer than she should have. "It was really good. Obviously, the man has had a lot of practice."

Liz grinned. "You like him."

"Not even a little bit," she denied. "He's a baseball player."

"Just because he has the same job as your father doesn't mean he's the same man," Liz pointed out.

"I know that. But why would I choose to get involved with a baseball player? They're on the road half the year. They're idolized by hundreds of thousands of people, so what does one woman matter? Not that I would even have that choice," she hastily added. "Matt Kingsley is just a celebrity participating in one of my fundraisers. He's like every other famous person I deal with."

"Is he really?" Kate prodded.

Judging by the looks on her friends' faces, she wasn't doing a very good job of convincing them that she felt nothing for the man.

But she did feel nothing, didn't she? So what if her lips still tingled from his kiss? One good kiss wasn't going to change anything.

"Let's talk about something else."

"Fine," Liz agreed. "But I have to say just one thing first."

"What's that?" she asked warily.

"Nobody is just one thing. Matt Kingsley may be a baseball player, but he's more than that. Before you count him out, maybe you should find out who he is as a man and not just what he does for his job."

"He's not interested in me," she protested. "This whole conversation is pointless. I told you it was a misunderstanding. That's all."

"We'll see," Kate said.

"What does that mean?" she asked in frustration.

"I'm just thinking if that one kiss has gotten you all worked up, Julie, maybe it did something to him, too."

* * *

Matt sat on his couch late Thursday night with a bag of ice strapped to his right shoulder and a laptop resting on his thighs as he waited for his brother to call. At twenty-five, Connor was a lieutenant in the Marine Corps and was currently stationed somewhere in the Middle East. While they didn't talk often, they did try to catch up every few months. Connor had emailed earlier that he wanted to talk tonight. Hopefully, he'd be able to make that happen, but he couldn't always get to the computer when he wanted to.

A moment later, the connection came through and Connor's face with his familiar grin filled the screen.

Matt couldn't help but smile back. No matter what Connor was doing, he always seemed able to find a reason to be happy, and considering the state of his life, Matt found that an even more amazing trait now than he ever had before. Connor had joined the Marines when he was nineteen, and he was six years into his eight-year contract. He'd been all over the world and while he'd had some minor injuries, he'd managed to make it this far without getting badly hurt or worse.

"What's with your arm?" Connor asked immediately.

"Nothing. Just icing."

"The season hasn't even started yet, and you're already hurting?"

"I'm fine. It was just the first day I've thrown in a while. I'm taking precautions."

"Well, you're not getting any younger," Connor reminded him. "Next year is the big 3-0."

"Thanks for the reminder. What's going on with you?"

"A lot actually. That's why I wanted to talk. I'm engaged, Matt."

His gut tightened at Connor's shocking news. "What? Who? I didn't even know you were seeing anyone."

"Her name is Ellen. She's a medic stationed over here. We've been going out about three months. She is beautiful and funny and brave, and has a body that is smoking hot.

She's everything—"

"That's great, but three months?" he interrupted, his mind grabbing onto the piece of information that made the least sense. "Why so fast?"

"It feels right, Matt."

"Yeah, because it's only been three months. Tell me you're having a long engagement at least."

"Sorry to disappoint you. We're planning to get married as soon as we can get leave together. Hopefully that will be within the next two months."

"What's the rush, Connor?"

"I'm in love."

"You fall in love all the time," he couldn't help pointing out. His brother had been breaking hearts since he was fifteen.

"This time is different." Connor's expression sobered. "I want you to be my best man, Matt. I know your schedule gets crazy during the season, but I need you to stand by my side. It will probably happen sometime in May. I'm going to do everything I can to plan it on an off-day for you or do it at night or something, because you have to there."

He wasn't as concerned about taking a day off during the season as he was about Connor's intention to get married so fast to a woman he barely knew. He didn't want to squelch his brother's enthusiasm but damn, how could he stand by and say nothing, do nothing, when Connor was making a huge mistake? "I really think you should take more time to get to know her."

"I know her, Matt. It may seem fast to you. But out here, doing what we do, seeing what we see, every day feels like three years. Everything is intense, bigger than life. You learn not to waste time, not to take tomorrow for granted. I love her. She loves me. We're keeping it simple."

His brother's words sent a shiver down his spine. While

he never actually forgot that his brother put his life on the line every day, he tried not to think about it.

"Just be happy for me," Connor added.

"You're making a mistake." He couldn't stop the words from leaving his mouth. "This is a big decision. You can't rush into marriage."

"Actually, I can. Look, I know you worry about me—about all of us—but I'm not a kid. I know what I'm doing."

Matt let out a sigh, knowing he was getting nowhere. "There's nothing I can say, is there?"

"No. If you want to worry about someone, focus on David. Last I heard, he's thinking of dropping out of college."

"What?" he asked, straightening up. "I just sent off his next tuition check."

Connor grinned. "I guess I just threw David under the bus. Tell him I'm sorry when you call to yell at him. Look, Matt, I have to go soon, so tell me how you're doing first."

"I'm—fine," he said, frustrated that their conversation was almost over and he hadn't managed to convince Connor of anything. "Have you talked to Mom?"

"Not yet, but I will. She's going to love Ellen. You all are."

"I'm sure she's great, but—"

"There is no but," Connor said, cutting him off. "When do you head down to Arizona for spring training?"

"Two weeks."

"How is your team shaping up?"

"We have a new pitcher who looks promising. But we'll see how he does when it counts."

"Anything else new with you? Met any good-looking women lately? Or is that a stupid question?"

Julie's pretty face flashed through his mind. His pause must have given something away, because his brother immediately jumped on his hesitation.

"There is someone," Connor said. "Tell me about her."

"There's nothing to tell. I met someone earlier today, but she could barely stand the sight of me."

"Sounds like a challenge to me," Connor said with a laugh. "What did you do to piss her off?"

"I play baseball, and she doesn't care for professional athletes, especially baseball players."

"So change her mind. You've got game."

"I might give it a shot," he said.

"When you give things a shot, you almost always win."

"Almost always," he echoed.

"My time is up, Matt," Connor said. "I'll email you about the wedding."

"Wait. Have you told Claire?" Maybe his super smart sister could convince Connor he was out of his mind.

"Not yet. We're going to talk this weekend. I'll tell her then."

"Or you could not tell her and think about the whole idea a little more," he couldn't help suggesting one last time. "Love doesn't have to be so fast."

Connor just laughed at him, the way he'd laughed at him so many other times in his life. But then Connor had had the luxury of not being the oldest, not being the man of the house, not having to worry about making sure everyone else was taken care of. Those concerns had fallen to Matt when his father passed away.

"What would you know about love?" Connor asked. "You haven't had a relationship that lasted longer than three weeks. Try something serious sometime and then talk to me."

"Goodbye Connor," he said. "Stay safe."

"Talk soon," Connor replied, then ended the connection.

Matt stared at the blank screen for a long minute,

Connor's words ringing through his head. Unlike Connor, he hadn't fallen in love every other second, and as his younger brother had reminded him, his relationships tended to end before they got off the ground. That was mostly his fault. He shied away from women who wanted too much. He had his hands full with keeping his career going, a career that was supporting everyone in his family.

Speaking of which…

He started another program on his computer and opened a video taken at the most recent batting practice. At some point, he'd acquired a hitch in his swing, and he needed to get it fixed before the season started. He needed to have another good year. At twenty-nine, he was starting to hear the clock ticking. But he had at least another five to eight years he told himself—as long as he didn't get hurt, as long as he didn't get distracted and lose his focus, as long as he didn't let a beautiful blonde get under his skin.

Julie's image moved through his head again.

They were meeting tomorrow night for his cooking lesson. That had probably been a bad idea. She was going to be a distraction. He should cancel.

On the other hand, he really wanted to see her again.

It was just one date. Then he'd get back to business.

Chapter Four

Friday night after work Julie met Matt at the door of the Brandon Street Supermarket. She'd been half-hoping he'd text her and call the whole thing off, but she hadn't heard a word from him.

She straightened as she saw him get out of his car and stride across the lot. Wearing jeans and a zip-up jacket over a dark t-shirt, he moved with confidence and graceful athleticism, and more than one woman gave him a second glance as he passed by. Matt didn't seem to notice the attention, his gaze sweeping the area until it settled on her. His lips curved into a smile, and he gave her a wave.

Her breath caught in her chest, and a shiver ran down her spine as he approached. He was a really attractive man with his wavy brown hair, tan skin and beautiful green eyes. And his broad, powerful shoulders and long, lean body made her stomach tighten. He was both a man's man and a woman's man, and no doubt thousands of kids looked up to him, too. That made him the perfect choice for a celebrity chef, but absolutely not the perfect choice for her.

But this wasn't a date; it was business. She was keeping the celebrity happy. She was protecting her event. She was doing it all for her company, she told herself.

But not even she completely believed that.

"You're late," she said, deciding to go on offense. Because being angry at Matt helped keep the warmer feelings at bay.

He glanced down at his watch and raised an eyebrow. "Three minutes."

She shrugged. "Late is late."

"Let's not waste any more time then," he said, waving her toward the entrance. "What are we making tonight?"

"I thought we'd go with scallops and a creamy risotto with a kale salad on the side. The prep isn't too difficult and the scallops cook quickly. Risotto can be a little tricky but it doesn't take long to cook. I hope you like fish or at the very least that you're not allergic to it."

"I do like fish and no food allergies, so it sounds like a good plan."

She grabbed a basket as they entered the store. "Great. I made out a list."

"I figured," he said with a small smile. "You seem like a planner."

"I'm a busy woman. I like to be efficient."

"It wasn't a criticism," he said lightly. "So what's first?"

"Let's get the scallops," she said, heading toward the butcher. "They're the centerpiece of the dish."

They'd barely made it to the fish counter when two young boys came running over to ask Matt for his autograph. He happily obliged, signing one's baseball cap and the other's t-shirt. Following the boys were a dad and two little girls, then two women, one with a baby, the other with a toddler. And then there was the beautiful redhead in the short skirt and high-heeled boots who told Matt he was her favorite player and wanted to take a selfie with him.

Judging by her tone, she wanted to do a lot more with Matt than just take a picture with him.

Julie got the scallops and headed off to finish the

shopping, leaving Matt with his fans. She should have anticipated this happening. Autograph seekers had often waylaid her father when they were out as a family. Her dad had always been happy to stop and talk with fans, just as Matt had done, but her mother had hated the constant interruptions. She couldn't really blame her. What started out as a task for two had often ended up as a task for one, just like today.

She picked up the rest of the groceries and then proceeded to checkout.

"There you are," Matt said, meeting her in line. "Sorry about that."

"It doesn't matter. Does this happen to you a lot?" she asked, as she unloaded her basket.

"In San Francisco, yes. Not so much other places. I'll pay for this," he added, moving past her to slide his credit card through the machine. "Did you get everything we need?"

"I think so."

"Thanks Julie." He gave her a smile that made her feel like an idiot for being pissed off at him because he was popular. It wasn't like he'd done anything to draw attention to himself. And it probably wasn't that fun for him to be accosted everywhere he went.

"No problem, but when we get to your place, you're going to be doing the cooking, and I'm going to be advising."

"And eating," he said. "Hopefully, it's good."

"Hopefully," she echoed, as they paid for their groceries and headed out to the parking lot.

She followed him to his condo, which was only about a mile away. He lived on the top floor of a sixteen-story brand new building overlooking the bay and the nearby ballpark.

After setting the bags down in the kitchen, Matt gave her a quick tour of the spacious two-bedroom, two-level unit.

The first floor was composed of the kitchen, dining room, living room, media room and bathroom. Upstairs were two master suites, each with their own bathrooms and sweeping views of the city. Also upstairs was a fitness room complete with treadmill, elliptical, weights and other fitness machines.

It was a great space, she thought. Everything was new, freshly painted, and there was no clutter anywhere.

"Your home is really nice," she said as they made their way back into the kitchen. "Have you lived here long?"

"No, I moved in about three months ago when the building was finished."

"I've never lived anywhere new. I grew up in a house that was fifty years old when my parents bought it, and the apartment building I live in now dates back to the nineteen-forties."

"My sister says this place has no soul," he said, stopping by the sink to wash his hands. "But everything is new."

"Well, I guess that's a little true," she said. "You just need to make the space more personal."

He shrugged. "I'm fine with it the way it is."

"How old is your sister?"

"Claire is twenty-three."

"Does she live nearby?"

"No, she's in medical school in Los Angeles."

"Really? That's a lot of work."

"It is a lot of work, but she's a great student and very determined. She wants to be a pediatrician. And I'm sure she'll make that happen. She's a force of nature."

"Sounds like that quality runs in your family," she said dryly. "You're a bit of a force yourself."

"Wait, was that a compliment?"

"Just a fact."

"Well, let's see how this force does in the kitchen. What's first?"

She started, realizing she'd forgotten all about cooking. She'd been far more interested in getting to know Matt than in producing a meal that would make him a contender in the cook-off. She took out her phone to review the recipe. "Why don't you grab a large saucepan for the risotto and a frying pan for the scallops. We'll also need to chop the mushrooms that will go into the risotto."

He opened a cupboard and took out some pans. "Will these work?"

"A bigger saucepan would be better," she said, watching as he exchanged pans. "At least you know what a saucepan is?"

"I'm somewhat familiar with what is used to cook, just not how to actually use it."

"Your mother didn't try to teach you at some point? Or were you just too busy with baseball?"

"My mother was more busy than I was. She worked two jobs for most of my childhood, so dinner often came out of the freezer. I can heat things up and use the microwave."

She paused, frowning as she realized she knew next to nothing about Matt Kingsley beyond his baseball reputation. "What was your mom's job?"

"She worked in retail sales during the day and for an office cleaning service at night."

"What about your dad?"

"He died when I was eleven," Matt replied, his eyes turning somber. "He'd gone sailing with some friends, the first time he'd done anything for himself in years. The boat got caught in a bad storm. It ended up breaking apart, and my dad didn't make it back to shore."

She stared at him in shock. He'd told the story pragmatically, but there was a pain in his eyes now that made her ache for him. "I'm so sorry, Matt. I had no idea that your father died when you were young."

"It isn't a subject I talk about much, although it's not a secret." He paused. "Right before his death, my father founded a startup computer company with a friend of his. Unfortunately, after my father died, his friend couldn't make the company work. He ended up losing everything my dad had invested in the business and then some. My mom had to sell our house to pay off my father's debts. Then we moved into a two-bedroom apartment that became home for the next six years. My mom had a room and then we had two sets of bunk beds in the other. When Claire needed more privacy, she ended up in my mom's room, and my mother would sleep on the couch."

She was really surprised by his story. She'd had no idea he'd gone through such a tragedy or had had a difficult childhood. "It sounds like a bad time. I'm kind of shocked I never heard any of that before."

"I don't talk about it much. My mother is a really private person, and she hated for anyone to know that my father had left her with so much debt. Once we moved away from the old neighborhood and started over, it was like having a new life, and we didn't talk much about the other. But I have a lot of respect for my mother. She went from being a stay-at-home mom raising four kids, to someone who had to find a way to support herself and the family. She rarely complained about it. She always had a great attitude and just kept telling us to move forward and not look back. We didn't have a lot of stuff or space in our lives, but there was a lot of love."

"Couldn't anyone help? What about your grandparents?"

"My mom's parents sent money when they could, but they weren't well-off. My dad's parents were older and sickly. They would also chip in at times, but it was really up to my mother to keep the ship afloat. I was the oldest, so I tried to step up—be the man of the family. Not that I knew what that meant when my dad died, but I did my best to contribute. I'd mow lawns, walk dogs, whatever the neighbors wanted done." He smiled. "I'm sure the few bucks I came up with were like pennies to my mom, but she always told me how proud she was of me, and she'd put the money I earned in a coffee can and said she was saving it for an emergency."

"I'm sure she was proud of you," Julie said, realizing that she felt a little proud, too. She probably should have done some research on Matt. She normally did that with the celebrities they worked with, but she'd been so fixated on the fact that he was a baseball player she hadn't looked beyond that. She hadn't wanted to know more, but now she did.

"When I graduated from high school," Matt continued. "My mother handed me the coffee can and told me to use the fourteen hundred and twenty-seven dollars I'd made over the last six years for school." He smiled at the memory. "I couldn't believe she'd never touched it. But she'd always felt bad that I was worrying about money instead of just being a kid."

"How old were your brothers and sisters when your father passed away?"

"Connor was eight, Claire was five and David was three."

"So they were all really young."

He nodded in agreement. "Yeah. It's hard to remember now a time when my dad was with all of us. David doesn't remember him at all. I used to feel badly for him, but sometimes I'm not sure that it isn't a good thing. He doesn't feel as much sadness for what he has no memory about."

"But you remember a lot, don't you?"

"Everything. It's a blessing and a curse," he said lightly. "So what do you want me to do with these pots?"

She started, realizing that she'd lost all track of what they were supposed to be doing—which was cooking.

"Just tell me what to do, and I'll do it," Matt added with a smile. "I'm all yours for the night, Julie."

His words sent a pack of butterflies dancing through her stomach, which was crazy, since the last thing she wanted was for him to be all hers. Wasn't it?

* * *

An hour and a half later, Matt sat back in his chair at the dining room table, having finished off the remarkably good dish he'd managed to cook with Julie's help. He couldn't remember the last time he'd had a home-cooked meal, and it certainly hadn't been here in his home. It felt good to eat in, to have a beautiful woman for company, to not have to be on for anyone. It was interesting, but with Julie, her candid dislike of his job and his fame, he actually found it easier to just be himself.

"Full?" she asked, spooning the last bite of scallop into her mouth.

"Stuffed. That was damn good. I must admit that I'm amazing."

She laughed at his cocky words. "And so humble, too. Let's not forget I was behind you every step of the way. So I'd say you were competent. Amazing is still a ways off."

"I'm not averse to some practice. We should do this again. In fact, I was thinking I should try another recipe, and then we can decide which one is better."

"Whoa. I think it would be better to just perfect this one. You only have a week." She started to get up, but he immediately waved her back into her seat. "You sit. I'll clean up."

"I was just going to take my plate to the sink, but fine. I'm happy to let you clean up. It's been a long day and an even longer week," she said.

"Let's go into the living room. The dishes can wait." He grabbed the bottle of wine off the table. "Bring your glass."

As she settled on the couch in the living room, he couldn't help thinking that he really liked this mellowed-out version of Julie Michaels. She was still in work clothes, black slacks and a teal-colored top, but she'd taken off her blazer while they were cooking, and her blonde hair fell loosely around her shoulders.

While her eyes were a little tired, they were still the prettiest blue he'd ever seen. And her lips were soft and tinged pink from the red wine she was sipping. He had an almost irresistible urge to kiss her. With any other woman, he would have sat down next to her and done exactly that. But he felt like he had to tread carefully when it came to Julie. She wasn't as bitter or as angry around now him, but she was still skittish, and he didn't want to scare her off.

He took a seat in the armchair adjacent to the couch. He'd had a hard week, too. Letting out a sigh, he tossed back the rest of his wine, then set his glass down and kicked up his feet on the coffee table.

"That was a big sigh," Julie commented, giving him a thoughtful look. "Rough week?"

"You could say that."

"But the season hasn't started yet. Shouldn't this be the easy part of the year for you?"

"Unfortunately the off-season now seems to be filled with other commitments. I spent the early part of the week in New York doing an ad campaign for jeans. I had to play model for two days. It was boring as hell and not my scene."

She suspected he'd looked pretty damn good in those jeans. "I'm sure you were paid well," she said.

"Very well. I actually have more respect for models now. It's not as easy as I thought it was. I was glad to get back on the plane, come home, and hit the practice field."

"Does your arm hurt, Matt?"

He realized he was subconsciously rubbing his right shoulder. "Yesterday was the first day I'd thrown in a month. It's a little tweaked, hopefully nothing more than that. I like to start the season off feeling healthy and strong. However, it's not just my arm that's bothering me though. I picked up a hitch in my swing, and it's pissing me off." He paused, frowning as he realized how small his problems must look to her. She worked hard to help people who were dealing with serious issues like hunger and homelessness. "I know—smallest violin in the world right?"

"Everyone's problems are important to them," she said, surprising him a little.

"That's a more generous response than I'd expect from you."

She shrugged. "We all get upset about petty things. I was really annoyed yesterday when I couldn't get a password to work on my computer. I had to take a breath and remind myself it's not that big of a deal." She tilted her head as she sipped her wine and gave him a long look. "Tell me something, Matt. You're a superstar, we both know that. You've set records, broken records, been named MVP, so do you really have that much left to prove?"

"I do," he said. "I need to put a few more good seasons under my belt before I run out the clock."

"You're only twenty-nine. You have a lot of time left. My father played until he was forty-one."

"He was lucky to stay healthy and that good that long." Matt was surprised she'd brought her father into the conversation.

"Yeah, my dad was always lucky."

He waited for her to continue, but that seemed to be all she wanted to say about her dad.

She took another sip of wine, then said, "How did you

get into baseball? Did your father play with you?"

He smiled at that thought. "No, my dad was not an athlete at all. He was a nerdy computer genius. However, my grandfather on my mom's side used to play, and he was the one to show me how to throw a ball. He loved baseball. When I was eight years old, we went on a family trip to Boston, and my grandpa took me to Fenway Park. I stood at the top of the stadium and looked down at the shiny diamond and then out at the fence they call the Big Green Monster and knew that one day I was going to hit a homerun over that very high wall. Being in that park was like walking through time. I could almost hear the sounds of the past, the old wood bats echoing the sound of every hit, the calls for beer and hotdogs. It was the most incredible place I'd ever seen."

He saw a light of recognition in her eyes. "You've been there, haven't you?"

She nodded. "Yeah, I know exactly what you mean about being able to hear the ghosts of the past there."

He could hardly believe they'd actually connected over something related to baseball.

"So your grandfather was the one who fueled your interest in the sport. Tell me more about the early days. Were you good from the very beginning? One of those kids who is just an outstanding athlete?"

"God, no," he said with a definitive shake of his head, remembering the struggle of his youth.

"Really?" she asked doubtfully.

"I grew late, Julie. When I was twelve and thirteen, I was a lot smaller than the competition. In a way, it worked in my favor. I couldn't depend on physical attributes to get the job done, so I had to be technically good at the mechanics of baseball. When I finally did pass the six-foot mark, I had excellent skills to back up my newfound size and power." He took a breath, choosing his words, wanting her to understand a little of where his passion came from. "It wasn't just my grandfather's love of the game that drove me on; the baseball field was a happy place for me, especially after my father died. I could forget about everything but the game for those two hours."

"That makes sense."

"And when I started to realize that I could be really good at the game, I saw baseball as my ticket to college. I knew there wouldn't be money to pay for that, so I would need a scholarship. That became my goal. And I worked really hard. I took more swings than anyone else. I was the first one to get to practice and the last one to leave. I had to play my way through obnoxious asshole coaches and team politics, but I just kept my head down and focused on getting the job done when I had the chance. By the time I was a junior in high school, I was breaking hitting records, pro scouts were calling me, and universities were offering me a full ride."

"Very impressive. I'm sure it helped to have natural talent to go along with your work ethic."

"Oh, it did. There is never just one thing that makes someone successful. It's always a combination."

"So you went to Stanford, right?"

"For a year, and then the scouts started offering me a lot of money to go pro. I couldn't pass up the opportunity. I spent a year in the minors. Then, by some miracle, I was pulled up to the Cougars starting lineup when their shortstop got injured. I've been there ever since."

"And you turned into a superstar," she said with a small smile.

"Not right away. But when we made it to the World Series three years ago, I had a fairly spectacular run at the plate, which helped my contract negotiations. And last year's run in the playoffs will hopefully help me out next year, but my contract will be up at the end of the season, and I want another one. It's never about what I did in the past but what I can contribute now and in the future that matters."

"Are you really that worried?"

"Let's just say I don't take it for granted."

"But even if it ended tomorrow or this year, you've obviously made a lot of money, achieved fame and you have a World Series ring. If it was over at the end of this season, wouldn't it have been enough?"

He thought about her question for a long moment. "I've asked myself the same thing," he said, meeting her gaze. "But it's not just about me, Julie. I support my mom and my siblings with that money. I need the income to last as long as possible so that everyone gets to where they need to go. I don't want to quit until I know I can walk away and everyone I care about will be fine. I also know that my career has an expiration date. In other professions, you can work into your seventies, but there's going to come a point where I have to figure out what to do next, and I'd like to push that point back as long as possible."

"That happened to my friend's boyfriend, Michael Stafford. His football career ended at twenty-five when he blew out his knee. He had to reinvent himself. He's doing well though."

"You have a friend that's a professional athlete, and you actually like them?"

She made a face at him. He's my friend's fiancé, and we all went to high school together, so I knew him before he was a superstar. Now, he's just a working guy like the rest of us. But getting back to you, I think it's really generous of you to take care of your family."

"I try. I bought my mother a house with a garden last year, which she loves. And I'm trying to help out my siblings, although sometimes that gets wearing, especially when they make stupid choices."

She raised an eyebrow. "Like what? Do you have an example?"

"Yes, I do. Connor is in the Marines. He called me last night to tell me he's getting married to a woman he met three months ago. He's always been impulsive, but this is crazy. They're going to get married when they both have a couple of days of leave, which means they're not even going to have time for a honeymoon. And he's in the middle of a war zone. What the hell is he thinking?"

"Maybe he's not thinking; he's just in love."

"He's always in love."

She smiled. "Obviously, he thinks this time is different."

"So he says, but he's being ridiculous. Why the rush? Why not wait? Date a while, survive deployment, and then get hitched?" He paused. "But Connor isn't my biggest concern at the moment. He's old enough to figure things out, but he told me last night that David, my youngest brother, wants to drop out of college. I just paid his tuition, and I can't even get him to text me back."

"They have to live their own lives, Matt. You had the chance to pursue your dreams. Why shouldn't they?"

"Because they're not being smart."

She laughed. "I'm sure they think they are."

"I'm sure they do, but they're not. You're lucky you don't have siblings."

She sucked in a quick breath, her face paling at his comment.

"What did I say?" he asked quickly.

"I do have siblings—two half-sisters. After my father left my mother and me, he had two girls with another woman. They're about eight and five now."

He realized now that he had heard about Jack's second family. He just hadn't really thought about it until this moment. "Have you met them?" he asked.

She shook her head. "No, I haven't seen my father in person since the night he told me he was leaving my mother."

He was shocked at her answer. "That's crazy. You're his kid, why wouldn't he see you?"

"I asked myself that, too. In the beginning, I didn't want to see him. He did tell my mother he wanted to come to my high school graduation, but I said absolutely not. The little contact my parents had during the divorce proceedings were always followed by three days of crying and anger and bitterness on my mom's part. I didn't want my graduation to put them anywhere near each other."

"I can understand why you wouldn't want to see him, but you have no interest in meeting your sisters?"

"They don't feel like they're anything to me," she replied. "I haven't even seen a photo. And my dad's second wife is five years older than me. It would feel so weird to see him with her." Julie shuddered at the thought. "I don't need any of that. It took me a long time to get past my father's betrayal."

"You know," he said carefully. "There are usually two sides to every divorce."

Her lips tightened. "And you're trying to suggest I don't know my father's side?"

"You just said you haven't seen him since you were a teenager. I'm guessing you haven't talked to him much, either."

"I didn't need to hear his side, Matt. I had a front row seat to his life. And even before the divorce, he wasn't around that much. My parents fought for a long time, and every fight ended with him leaving, because he had a game to go to. He always said, 'I can't do this right now'. But a better time never seemed to materialize. So yes, I took my mom's side in the divorce. How could I not? He didn't just leave my mom; he cheated on her. And it wasn't just once."

"It sounds like they were unhappy for a while."

"Because he put baseball before everything else."

"Can you really blame it all on baseball?"

"It was my father's whole life, Matt. Just as I'm sure it's your whole life."

"I have time for family," he protested.

"Then you're a better man than my dad."

"How long were your parents together?"

"A long time. They met when they were eighteen. My mom supported my father through years in the minors. And when it came to the family, the house, she did everything. He wasn't there in the middle of the night when I got sick, but she was. And when he needed her, she was there for him, too. What did she get for her loyalty? Nothing." She let out a breath. "I can still here the dismissive tone in his voice when he said there was nothing to do but get a divorce, as if it wasn't his fault that he didn't love her anymore. You know Jack Michaels the hero; you don't know the man."

She had a point. "I don't know what Jack was like as a husband or a father, but I do know what he was like as a teammate, as a mentor."

"You should stop there, Matt. You're not going to change my mind about him. I don't care that he was nice to you or the other ballplayers. That's great for all of you, but my experience was different." She set her wine glass down. "I should go."

"We can change the subject."

"Can we?" she asked with a sigh. "With you, it's always going to come back to baseball. You live a life that I have no interest in knowing about. I don't really know why I'm even here. Do you?"

Chapter Five

"That's harsh," he said, her words cutting to the bone.

"I'm being honest, Matt."

"Then let me be honest, too. There's a spark between us. I felt it when we kissed yesterday; I think you did, too."

Her eyes brightened at his words. "Even if that were true, and I'm not saying it is, it doesn't matter. I could never date a baseball player."

"You do know that bad husband/father behavior isn't just for ballplayers, right? If your father was an accountant, would you paint all accountants as losers?"

"I doubt my father would have had as many opportunities to cheat if he were an accountant, and don't pretend you haven't seen your fellow ballplayers cheat on their girlfriends or wives."

"I've seen guys cheat, but they weren't all ballplayers. That's my point."

"So your point is that all guys cheat," she countered.

"You're twisting my words."

"Am I?"

He let out a sigh. "So what would it take for a man to convince you he's trustworthy?"

"I honestly don't know. Maybe I'll just end up alone with a couple of cats. Actually, I don't really like cats, so let's make that a dog." She blew out a sigh. "I know you think I'm a head case, and maybe I am. I actually haven't talked this much about my father or my past in years. It's just you and your profession that brought it all up."

"So the guys you've been going out with have no clue just how high a bar they have to reach?"

"I wouldn't say there have been a lot of guys."

"But some…"

"I did go out with an interesting man last week, and we have a second date set up. He runs a non-profit in Marin County."

"A do-gooder like yourself. Sounds like just the right guy."

"I do good, but I am not a do-gooder," she protested. "Or if I am, so what? Why is that a bad thing?"

"It's not bad. It's just frustrating to be judged by your career, isn't it? You don't like being called a do-gooder, just like I don't appreciate being painted as a cheater who doesn't know how to treat a woman or how to be faithful."

"Have you ever cheated, Matt?"

"No," he said flatly.

She stared back at him. "You've never been tempted?"

"If I were dating a woman and I was tempted by someone else, I'd break things off."

"You didn't answer my question though. I asked if you'd ever been tempted."

He thought for a moment. "That would be a no."

"Have you been in a serious relationship recently?"

"That would also be a no."

"Well, maybe that's why you haven't been tempted. You haven't committed to anyone, so it doesn't matter what you do."

"I take commitment seriously. I don't make one unless I can back it up. What about you, Julie?"

"I feel the same way," she returned. "And I'm very committed to my work. I need to make things happen in my career as much as you need to have another great season. I don't have a family to support, but I do have to take care of myself. I don't ever want to end up like my mother. She didn't work the whole time my parents were together and then she ended up not knowing how to do anything, needing him to give her support just so she could survive. That's never going to be me."

"Where does your mom live now?" he asked curiously.

"Sunnyvale."

"How is she doing?"

"She's fine. She actually remarried three months ago. He's a psychologist, which is probably good, because she has even more baggage than I do."

He smiled, appreciating the fact that Julie could acknowledge that her feelings were a little off base. "Do you like him?"

"I do. I don't know him that well. He's kind of quiet, and he often seems to be watching me, analyzing me, but I give him credit for never offering his opinion. He seems to treat my mother well, and that's what really matters. She's happy, and to be honest, I wasn't sure she ever would be."

"Interesting," he said. "So your mom got over her anger and bitterness against men to marry again."

"Or she's just making another mistake, and it's too soon to know. They haven't been together very long."

"You're really a glass-half-empty kind of woman, aren't you?"

She made a face at him. "Only when it comes to love and professional athletes. I'm pretty optimistic in other parts of my life."

"That remains to be seen."

"You don't have to see anything. We're just ships

passing in the night."

"We're going to be in the same hemisphere for at least the next ten days," he countered.

"I do appreciate your supporting the cook-off, Matt. I'm sure you'd rather have your focus completely on baseball, but your efforts will help a lot of people, I can promise you that. The Foundation does really excellent work. It takes very little money for overhead. The majority of funds go to the actual programs that we support."

"Sounds like you don't have a big salary."

"No, I definitely do not have that, but I do get a lot of satisfaction from my work."

He liked that she was passionate about her job. He'd always found women who had something else going on in their lives to be the most interesting. "Did you always want to work for a non-profit?"

"No. Like most people, I had no clue what I wanted to do with my life. I was an English major in college. I liked to read and write, but I didn't think I could make a living with that. When I got out of college, I saw an ad for a promo assistant at a non-profit, and I was lucky enough to get it. The pay was terrible. The hours were long, but the people were great. I learned a lot, and I started to realize how rewarding it was to actually work towards something that would make someone else's life easier. So I guess you could say I kind of fell into it. Now I love the job, but it's not easy. There are a lot of nonprofits competing for the same dollars, and I've never been great at wrangling money."

"Just reluctant ballplayers," he teased.

She smiled. "I have been somewhat successful at getting celebrities, but that's because I shamelessly use my connections. I've also gotten really lucky in the last year because two of my friends have fallen in love with some very well connected men. Michael Stafford, who I mentioned earlier, has helped me get some football players for our upcoming telethon. And my friend Andrea just married Alex Donovan. I don't know if you've heard of him—"

"I know Alex. He's a huge baseball fan. He's been my guest at the park a few times. Why isn't he cooking at your event?"

"He's already participated in a couple of other fundraisers and he has his own foundation to run, so I try not to overstep with too many requests. Alex and Michael have both bought tickets for the event, so you'll see them there."

"And hopefully I won't poison anyone."

"I feel pretty good, so I'm confident your entry will be well received by the judges."

"You helped me a lot," he reminded her. "Am I going to get the same help at the event?"

"No. I will have a ton of things to do that night, so you might want to make the dish again before then." She paused, glancing down at her watch. "I should go. I have a walkathon meeting early tomorrow."

"When is the walkathon?"

"In two weeks. We have a lot of events and not enough staff to run them all."

"I'm beginning to see that."

She got to her feet. "This was more fun than I expected."

He laughed. "I guess I'll take that as a compliment." He walked her to the door. "Thanks again, Julie. I do appreciate the time you gave me tonight. In fact, I'd like to take you out to dinner to repay you."

She hesitated. "I'm sorry but I can't."

"You're really turning me down?" Despite her honest admission that she didn't care for baseball players, he was still shocked that she'd said no.

"First time?" she teased.

"In a while," he admitted.

"I already have a date for tomorrow."

"With environmental guy?"

She nodded. "Yes."

"What about Sunday?"

"Sunday night I'm taking a hip-hop dancing class at my friend Isabella's studio. If you want to join me for the class, we could get some food afterwards."

He stared at her in disbelief. "You want me to do hip-hop dancing with you? Seriously?"

She laughed. "It's a great workout, good for coordination, balance, sweating out the toxins, and it's fun. You wouldn't be the only guy there, in case you're worried."

"I'm never worried about being the only guy anywhere," he retorted.

"Then what do you say?"

"What time should I pick you up?"

"I could meet you there."

"Let's go together. Text me your address."

"All right."

He followed her to the front door. She opened it, then paused. "What you said before about me was true—I am a lot of work, Matt. I'm sure you could find plenty of women who are a lot easier to be around."

He knew he could. But he'd done easy. And difficult was far more interesting. "I'll see you Sunday."

* * *

After suffering through a rather boring Saturday evening date, Julie had woken up Sunday morning with Matt on her mind. Actually, he'd been on her mind since the first moment they'd met, since he'd impulsively kissed her in the parking lot and then charmed her the next evening with stories about his family.

There was certainly more to him than she'd first thought, and she was excited and a little nervous to see him again, even though she was absolutely certain that going out with him was a bad idea. She pulled a lightweight jacket over her tank top and leggings and checked her front window for his car. There was no sign of the bright red Ferrari. She let the curtain fall and paced around her living room, trying to burn off some restless energy.

She needed to figure out how to handle Matt—or more importantly how to handle herself.

She'd wanted to feel sparks for Eric, the very nice guy she'd gone out with the night before. But their second date hadn't gone as well as their first, and that was Matt's fault. Matt, with his bigger-than-life personality, his wicked green eyes and sexy smile had made Eric pale in comparison. Eric was attractive, but he wasn't in Matt's league. And why would he be? He sat behind a desk most days and his pale skin probably burned if he got into the sun. But Eric was responsible, committed to his cause of protecting the environment. He cared about making the world a better place, and he was exactly the kind of man she should like.

She obviously had too much of her mother in her. Instead of making the sensible choice, she was being tempted by a man who could easily break her heart.

Her phone rang, interrupting her worrisome thoughts. Was it Matt calling to bail out of class? She grabbed the phone out of her bag and saw her mother's name.

"Hi Mom," she said. "I was just thinking about you."

"I was thinking about you, too," Alicia Michaels replied. "How are you, honey? It's been a few weeks since we've spoken."

"I hadn't realized." That wasn't completely true. Since her mom had gotten remarried, they hadn't talked as often as they used to.

"Are you free for dinner tonight?" her mom asked. "I thought that Kent and I might drive up to the city and take you out. I know it's last minute, but I wasn't sure of Kent's plans until now."

Her mother's words made Julie frown. Why did her mom always let a man's plans take precedent over her own? Or was she once again painting men with her dad's old brush?

"I'm sorry," she said. "I'm just about to go to a hip-hop class with some friends. I can't cancel this late."

"Oh, of course. I understand. Maybe next weekend."

"I don't know, Mom. It's crazy busy right now at work. We have a couple of big events coming up over the next few weekends."

"Well, let's try to make time somewhere. I miss you, Julie. It was just you and me for so many years. It's strange not to talk to you every day."

"I know, Mom. I feel the same way. But you're happy with Kent, right?"

"I am, more than I ever imagined I would be. He's a really wonderful man. I never thought I could fall in love after your father did what he did, but Kent is so different, so attentive. Even when we sleep, he has his hand on me. It's like he can't bear to be too far from me at any moment."

Julie's heart turned over. She really was happy for her mother, maybe a little jealous, too. "I'm so glad, Mom. You deserve to have a man like that."

"I want you to have one, too."

"I'm not worried about that. I have lots of time."

"I feel like I may have poisoned you a little when it comes to men. I've been feeling guilty about all the ranting and raving I did about your father when you were younger."

"You didn't tell me anything I didn't see with my own

eyes. So don't worry about it." Her apartment buzzer rang. "I have to go Mom. We'll talk soon."

"Call me back tomorrow. There's something else I want to discuss with you. It concerns your father."

Her gut tightened. "What about him?" She pressed a button to let Matt in. She'd been intending to run down to greet him, but now she was distracted by her mom's cryptic words. "What's going on, Mom?"

"I can't get into it if you're on your way out the door. Call me tomorrow and we'll talk."

"Okay," she said reluctantly. "Bye Mom."

She ended the call and opened her door. Matt stood before her in a navy blue t-shirt and gray workout sweats. He looked good no matter what he wore. He gave her a smile that made her toes curl. Yeah, going out with him again was a really bad idea.

"Julie," he said in his deep baritone. "Are you ready?"

"I am. Just let me grab my keys."

"No hurry," he replied, following her into the apartment.

Her very small one-bedroom apartment would probably fit into his living room, but she didn't care. She loved her warm, cozy space, and the rent had been a steal. A friend of her mother's owned the place and had been transferred to London, so she needed a subletter. Julie had jumped at the chance to move out of the apartment she shared with three friends and have some space of her own. Not that she didn't miss the girls, but living by herself was really great.

"It's nice," Matt said, his gaze sweeping the room. "Not quite what I expected."

"What do you mean?"

"It's…girly."

"I am a girl," she said dryly.

He smiled. "Since we've met I've seen mostly your sharp side. Now there appears to be a lot more softness to you, even some whimsy, and a hell of a lot of pillows," he said, waving his hand toward the six colorful pillows taking up most of her couch.

"I like color," she said.

"And flowers." He paused by a side table to study a big bouquet of daisies. "Unless these are from your date last night?"

"No, I bought them for myself. One of my former roommates runs a small flower shop near my office. I stop in there at least once a week. I like flowers and pillows, but the owner of this place is responsible for the purple walls." She grabbed her keys off the kitchen counter. "We can go now."

"I haven't seen the bedroom."

"Maybe another time."

"I like the sound of that."

"You know I didn't mean it like that." She waved him toward the door. They walked down the three flights of stairs together and made their way out to the sidewalk. The afternoon sun had disappeared into a mass of thick, foggy clouds. She shivered and zipped up her jacket.

"The weather changes fast in this city," Matt commented as he opened the car door for her.

"I like the fog. Mother nature's air conditioner."

"I don't mind it, except when it creeps into the ballpark, and I lose the fly ball in the mist." He frowned. "And I'm bringing up baseball again."

"It's a big part of your life," she murmured.

"I was going to try not to talk about it tonight."

"Well, we won't be doing much talking at dance class. And you don't have to try not to talk about your life. We both know what you do for a living."

"And we both know it bothers you. So tonight we'll dance and talk about other things." He shut her door, then walked around the car and slid behind the wheel. "Speaking of dancing, am I going to look like an idiot in this class?"

"I don't know. Are you a good dancer?"

"I'm really good at tapping my foot to the beat while standing in a bar. Does that count?" he asked as he started the car.

She smiled. "I don't think so. But you have a lot of natural athletic talent, so I suspect you're better than you think. And it doesn't matter if you're not. You'll like the workout and Isabella is great at getting everyone in the class involved. She's a fantastic teacher and wait until you see her moves. She's really good. She's been in music videos and danced at the Grammy's."

"Sounds like we're in good hands then. Is Isabella a friend as well as a dance teacher?"

"Yes, she's one of my best friends. I lived with her up until a few months ago. We met in college. In fact, I found most of my closest friends freshman year in a communal bathroom. We've all stayed pretty close over the years. In fact, we have a pact that no matter how far we drift apart, we'll always come back for each other's weddings. It sounded like a great idea in theory, but lately my friends have been getting engaged every other month, so I feel like I'm on a merry-go-round of bridal showers and bachelorette parties."

"I've had a few friends tie the knot in the last couple of years, too. Fortunately, I only had to usher in one of those weddings."

"Are your friends all ballplayers?" she asked curiously.

"A lot of them are, but I do have one good friend from childhood that I still see. He's an orthopedic surgeon now."

"Maybe he could give you an opinion on your arm."

Matt shot her a smile. "He has. He told me to stop throwing so hard or so often. Obviously, that's not an option."

"You should be careful. You don't want to end up with a serious injury."

"I have a lot of trainers looking out for me."

"Sure," she said, having forgotten for a moment that Matt did not need her to worry about him. He had an entire team of people who were there to support every aspect of his career and probably the rest of his life as well. Their lives were very, very different, and she really shouldn't let herself forget that.

Chapter Six

The dance studio was located in a one-story brick building near the flower mart. As he parked his car in the shadowy lot, Matt wondered just what he'd gotten himself into. Not just because the area was a little run-down, but also because he was stepping completely out of his world. He spent most of his time at the ballpark or the gym or with baseball friends, and it was only since he met Julie that he was beginning to realize how isolating his life had become.

"Don't worry," Julie said. "The neighborhood looks worse than it is. Your car will be safe."

"I'm not worried about my car," he said.

"Really?" she asked doubtfully as she got out of the car. "It's pretty fancy."

He smiled. "I won it, Julie. It was the MVP gift in last year's playoffs. Before that I was driving a ten-year-old jeep."

"You've certainly upgraded. It goes with your celebrity."

"It's just a car. I've never been that into what I drive."

"Then why not trade it in for a less sportier vehicle?"

"You might find this surprising, but I can be a little lazy."

"Except when it comes to baseball, right?"

He tipped his head to her point. "Right."

"Well, you won't be able to be lazy tonight. Isabella will kick your ass."

"Does she own this place?"

"Her aunt is the owner, but Isabella is the manager. They have two studios and all kinds of classes ranging from ballet to hip-hop. In the daytime, they work with more serious professional dancers and at night, Isabella runs classes to bring in the rest of us." She paused as another car pulled into the lot. "There's Michael and Liz. Let's wait for them."

He was happy to see another guy in the mix. Even though Julie had told him there would be men there, he hadn't been entirely convinced. Since Michael Stafford was an ex-pro-football player, they also had something in common.

"Hi guys," Julie said as Michael and Liz got out of the car. "I want you to meet Matt Kingsley. This is my friend Liz Palmer and her fiancé Michael Stafford."

"I've seen you play," Matt said, extending his hand to Michael. "Nice to meet you."

"Likewise," Michael said with a warm smile. "So how did you get talked into this?"

"I wanted to see Julie again, and this is what she was doing," he said simply.

Michael laughed and shook his head. "The things we do for women."

"It's going to be fun," Julie said. "Let's go inside. I think it's almost time for class to start."

"Have you done this before?" Matt asked Michael as they walked into the studio.

"Not hip-hop, but Liz did make me take a ballroom dance class a few weeks ago."

"Which you sucked at," Liz said with a teasing smile.

He gave a cheerful nod. "It's true. I had great moves on the football field, but the dance floor I seemed to trip over myself every two seconds. Although part of the problem was that this woman here likes to lead instead of follow," he added, putting his arm around Liz and giving her a squeeze.

"Because I knew what I was doing and clearly you did not," Liz protested.

Michael laughed. "You always say that." He looked at Matt. "We've been fighting since we were fourteen years old. High school rivals."

"Really? And that turned into love?"

"It was always love," Julie put in. "They were just too stubborn and competitive to see it when they were teenagers. Trust me, I know. I was there. I heard Liz rant about Michael more nights than I can count."

"That's true. Michael was a pain in my side," Liz agreed. "But then we grew up and figured out those sparks between us were more about love than hate."

"Exactly right," Michael said, giving Liz a quick kiss. Then he pulled open the door. "Let's dance."

The large studio with slick hardwood floors and a wall of mirrors was filled with about a dozen people when they entered. Isabella immediately came over to greet them with a happy smile and a quick hug for her girlfriends. With her dark eyes and dark hair, she had an exotic beauty but it was her infectious smile that really charmed Matt.

Within minutes they were lining up, and Isabella was giving some brief instructions on what they were going to do.

"Ready?" Julie asked as Isabella went to start the music.

"Probably not," he said. "But we'll soon find out."

"Everyone is learning, so we're all in the same boat."

"Yeah, but there seem to be a few more eyes on me," he said, tipping his head toward the mirror where a couple of women had clearly recognized him.

Julie gave him a dry smile. "I doubt you could do

anything that would wipe the interest out of their eyes."

"You seem to think I have no trouble getting women."

"Do you?"

"Well right now, I seem to be going to a lot of trouble just to spend time with you."

"I still haven't figured out why you're going to that trouble. You're not going to change my mind."

"We'll see," he said, speaking more confidently than he felt. But believing he could do something, no matter how impossible it was, had always worked for him before. Hopefully, it would this time.

* * *

Julie watched Matt in the mirror as they danced to the music, and she wasn't alone. As Matt had commented earlier, there were a lot of eyes on him, but he was holding his own. He followed directions well, and he had a natural rhythm.

He caught her watching him and smiled. She immediately looked away. She'd shivered a little at the purposeful look in his eyes when he'd told her he was going to change her mind about him. The more she challenged him, the more he wanted to show her that she was wrong and he was right. If she started gazing at him with adoring eyes, telling him how wonderful he was and saying she'd date him any place any time, he probably wouldn't be that interested.

Obviously, she'd played him all wrong.

Only she hadn't been playing; she'd just been honest and that had somehow increased Matt's interest in her. He enjoyed challenges and he was driven to win.

But he wasn't going to win her.

She might like him more than she'd expected to, but bottom line there could never be anything serious between them, not with her history. She had a lot more to lose than just a firmly entrenched opinion about baseball. She couldn't put her heart on the line and have another ballplayer break it.

Forcing thoughts of Matt out of her head, she concentrated on the dance, putting all of her energy into every move, so that she could get rid of the restless desire that seemed to course through her whenever she got close to Matt.

An hour later the class ended. She grabbed a drink of water as Matt took a towel from Isabella and wiped off his sweaty face.

"You were very good," Isabella told Matt. "Nice moves for a beginner. And you weren't bad either, Julie. You have the second dance down."

"Thanks, you're a great teacher."

"I agree," Michael said as he and Liz joined them. "I worked up a sweat and an appetite. Who wants to go out for pizza? My treat."

"I wish I could go," Isabella said with an apologetic smile. "But I have a family thing. Maybe next Sunday—if you guys come back for another class."

"You're on," Michael said. He turned to Julie and Matt. "What about you two?"

Before she could answer, Matt jumped in. "Sounds good to me. I'm starving."

"Great," Liz said, obviously happy with Matt's answer. "We can all get to know each other better." She sent Julie a pointed look. "Right Jules?"

"Okay," Julie said, knowing she didn't have much choice but to agree. And there was no danger in a group, right? Pizza and beer—what could go wrong?

* * *

An hour later, Julie knew exactly what could go wrong.

Seated in a corner booth at Vincenzo's with Matt, Liz and Michael, Julie had quickly become the focus of the conversation as Matt pressed Liz for information about Julie.

"Tell me what Julie was like in high school?" Matt asked.

Liz smiled. "Well, Julie and I were kind of outside the popular group."

"Kind of?" Julie echoed.

Liz made a face of her, then turned to Matt. "I was really intense. I liked to run for office a lot, even though I usually lost to Michael, who was the star athlete and the most popular kid in the class."

"What can I say?" Michael said with a helpless shrug.

"Nothing, so you can be quiet," Liz told him. "Julie was part of the uncool band kid group."

"Oh, yeah?" Matt asked, turning to her with new interest in his eyes. "What did you play?"

"The flute," she said.

"Was it a marching band?"

"On occasion."

"Do you still play?"

"Not often."

"I had no idea you played an instrument," he mused. "Interesting."

She had no idea why he thought that was interesting, but then he'd been looking at her all evening like she was a puzzle he had to figure out. Apparently, Liz had just given him another piece of the puzzle.

"Oh my God," Liz said suddenly.

"What?" Julie asked, surprised and wary of the eager light in Liz's face.

"I just had a phenomenally good idea. You should play at our wedding. I've been wanting to have an instrumentalist, and I was thinking guitar, but a flute would be pretty, and you are so good."

"I haven't practiced seriously in years," she protested.

"You'll get it right back, I'm sure," Liz said confidently.

"No, it's too much pressure. If I screwed up, I'd ruin your wedding. I think you should hire a professional."

"Our wedding is going to be a small affair with family and close friends. I would much rather have you play something than a stranger."

"But I'm going to be your maid of honor," she reminded Liz.

"You could do both. Just one or two songs before the ceremony starts. It would really mean a lot to me, and you owe me, Jules. I listened to you practice a lot in high school and college, too. Let's not forget that you had thoughts of joining an orchestra at one point."

"So music was more than a childhood passion?" Matt questioned.

"I had thought about playing in an orchestra, but I wasn't good enough." She turned back to Liz. "I'll think about it. But no promises."

"I'll take that for now, but we are going to keep talking about it," Liz said.

Knowing the level of Liz's stubbornness, Julie thought it would probably be a good idea to pull out her flute very soon.

"What about guys?" Matt asked Liz. "Did Julie have any notable high school boyfriends?"

"You know I'm right here," Julie interrupted.

"Yeah, but you're not going to tell me anything," Matt said with a grin. "I think Liz will give me more information."

"There is no information," Julie said. "I didn't have any boyfriends in high school. Tell him, Liz."

"What about Shawn Parker?" Liz asked.

"He was my biology lab partner. The only thing he was

interested in was whether I would dissect the frog when he got grossed out."

"That's true. But you did take him to that one dance."

"Only because I didn't want to sit at home and be a total loser," she retorted. "But he was definitely not my boyfriend."

"Okay, I'll agree with that," Liz said. She looked at Matt. "Julie didn't have a boyfriend, but she did have a lot of guys who were interested in her. She just didn't realize it."

"You are so lying," Julie said.

"No, she's not," Michael put in. "I know a lot of guys who wanted to date you, but they were afraid to ask you. You had a definite hands-off vibe about you, especially senior year."

Which had been after her dad left. That entire year had passed in a blur of pain and anger.

"Julie always thought that the guys only wanted to talk to her because she was Jack Michaels' kid," Liz interjected.

"That was the reason most of them were interested," she said. "They thought I could get them tickets, or I could hook them up with my dad's agent. It didn't matter that my dad had divorced my mother. They were still convinced I could do something for them. When they finally figured out I couldn't or wouldn't, they quickly disappeared."

"Not all of the guys were like that," Liz said quietly. "But you were anti-men for a while there."

She shrugged, knowing that Liz was right, but what did it matter now?

"I know what it feels like to have people use you to get ahead," Matt said, giving her a compassionate look. "I'm sure Michael does, too. I'm sorry you went through that Julie."

"Thanks," she said, surprised and touched by his words. A look passed between them that went on far too long, but she couldn't seem to drag her gaze away from Matt. Was it possible that this guy she should hate actually understood her better than anyone else?

Liz cleared her throat. "We're going to get going. I have to finish up some work before my early call tomorrow. Will we see you guys next week?"

"I should be able to come," she said. "I'm not sure Matt wants to repeat the class."

"I'll see what my schedule is," Matt said. "I wouldn't mind doing it again. It was more fun than I expected."

"Matt, it was great to meet you. I hope to see more of you in the future," Liz said. She gave him a pointed smile. "Don't let Julie scare you off."

Matt smiled back at Liz. "I don't scare easily.

Julie sighed. "Again, I'm right here."

Liz laughed. "Bye. Talk to you soon."

"Goodnight," she said, giving Michael a smile as he followed Liz out of the restaurant. She turned back to Matt. "Are you ready to go?"

"Sure."

"I'm glad you enjoyed the class," she said, as they walked down the street. "Or were you just saying that to be nice?"

"I never say what I don't mean," he told her.

"Never? You make a lot of big claims, Matt. You don't break promises. You don't say what you don't mean…"

He put his hand on her arm, stopping her in the middle of the sidewalk. "Maybe I feel the need to be direct, because it's clear you don't trust me."

"I don't know you well enough to trust you."

"That's why we're spending time together."

"Is that why?" she asked, feeling a little bewildered by it all.

"Well, there's this, too."

He lowered his head and covered her mouth with his.

Chapter Seven

Matt's hot breath mixed with the cold night air and all Julie wanted to do was get closer to the heat. He kissed the way he did everything else—with focus, energy and determination to get it right—and it certainly felt right. His lips were firm, his tongue a devilish delight, and the way he slid that tongue in and out of her mouth made her heart pound against her chest.

He angled his head to gain better access, and she went with him, kissing him back with a fervor that surprised herself. But she'd wanted another kiss since the last one they'd exchanged. And even if it was stupid and reckless, she couldn't seem to stop herself from tangling her tongue with his and letting desire and emotion take over.

Kissing Matt was like getting on a runaway train. The thrills kept building, but at some point she started to worry what would happen in the end.

Would they crash or would one of them be able to throw on the brakes at the last minute? And would that person be her?

It turned out to be Matt who lifted his head first, who stared down at her with intense, glittering eyes that told her just how much he wanted her.

She drew in a gulp of air as she tried to catch her breath.

Matt's hands fell from her waist as he stepped away and ran a hand through his hair in what appeared to be bewilderment. "That was…"

She waited somewhat breathlessly for him to finish that sentence, but he couldn’t seem to find the word he wanted. "Amazing, fantastic, unbelievable," she prodded.

He smiled. "All of the above."

"Yes," she agreed. After the way she'd kissed him, there was no point in trying to pretend she wasn't attracted to him. "But we can't do it again."

"Why not?"

"You know why," she said, waving a vague hand in the air.

"Are you really going to let my job stop you from going out with me?" he asked. "Haven't we moved past that?"

"We can never move past it. And while the ride with you might be really fun and exciting, I know what happens at the end."

You're jumping ahead, Julie. We're just having fun. Tonight doesn't have to be the start or the end of anything. It's just tonight. Live in the moment."

It was hard to argue with logic, but she knew they were only postponing the inevitable.

Matt turned his head toward the sound of music wafting down the street. "Let's go check that out."

"I'd rather just go home," she said, but Matt was already walking down the street.

She jogged a little to catch up with him and then followed him into a dimly lit bar where a female folk singer strummed a guitar and sang about love and heartbreak. The woman was good, and the music seemed more than a little appropriate Julie thought. Maybe they should listen to the music. Maybe they should pay attention to the lyrics, too.

"Let me buy you a drink," Matt said. "It's still early."

"All right." As much as she knew she needed to say goodbye to Matt, she wasn't quite ready.

They sat down at a table and ordered two beers while they listened to the singer. The bar was only half-full, and all attention was on the woman whose smoky voice commanded attention.

"She's really good," Matt said when the woman paused between songs to grab a bottle of water.

"She is," Julie agreed. "She has a soulful tone to her voice. It's pretty."

"Tell me about your former music ambitions."

"You already heard pretty much the whole story."

"I don't think I did. Liz mentioned that when you were playing in college, you wanted to get into an orchestra. Why didn't that happen?"

"I wasn't good enough."

He stared back at her, doubt in his eyes.

"What? You don't believe me?" she challenged.

"You don't seem like a woman who just quits."

"Sometimes you have to accept reality. Not every little boy who dreams of being a professional baseball player makes it to the big leagues. And not every girl who plays the flute makes it into a professional orchestra. Some dreams don't come true."

Her words only deepened his frown.

"I'm not being negative," she said defensively. "I'm just practical. Sometimes chasing an impossible dream is a waste of time."

"Is that being practical or being afraid of putting it all on the line?" he challenged.

"It's being practical," she said, refusing to let his question sway her. "It's not about fear. It's about playing the cards you're dealt."

"I don't agree."

"Then we'll have to agree to disagree." She settled back into her seat as the woman began to sing again, grateful for the interruption. Even though she'd told Matt she didn't agree with him, his words had gotten into her head. She didn't need him questioning her decisions. She was doing all right for herself. Maybe it would have been cool to play in a professional orchestra, but she liked the job she had now. She wasn't going to waste another minute thinking about *what ifs*. There was just no point to regret. It didn't change anything.

The music gradually seeped into her soul, lessening her tension, slowing her pulse. Music had always been her escape, and tonight was no different. By the time they left the bar, she was feeling a lot calmer.

The trip back to her apartment was made in relative quiet. Matt insisted on parking and walking her inside. She should have liked his attentiveness, but the closer they got to her apartment, the more she worried about saying goodnight—or not saying goodnight. She could ask him in. She could hook up with him. It would be amazing; she knew that. But she wasn't that kind of girl. She didn't start relationships that couldn't possibly go anywhere. And she didn't want to have sex with a man she probably wouldn't see again after the cook-off. She knew herself. And getting that close to a man would involve her emotions. Once those got into the mix, she could get hurt, and she was not going to let Matt hurt her.

She unlocked her door and stepped inside, turning on the lights as she did so. Then she turned back to Matt, who hovered in the doorway.

For a long minute they just looked at each other. Then she said, "I had fun tonight."

"I'm glad you can admit that at least. I did, too."

"I guess the next time I'll see you will be the cook-off."

"I have a feeling I'll see you before then."

"I'm pretty busy—"

"And you're afraid if we spend time together, you won't be able to keep your hands off of me," he said with a cocky note in his voice.

He was absolutely right, but there was no way she was going to tell him that. "Goodnight, Matt," she said pointedly.

"No kiss?"

"Apparently, I can keep my hands off of you," she said dryly, crossing her arms in front of her chest.

He laughed. "I walked right into that one, didn't I?" He quickly bridged the gap between them and stole a quick kiss before she could uncross her arms and push him away. "Goodnight, Julie. I'll see you soon."

* * *

She wasn't going to call him, wasn't going to see him, wasn't going to think about him, Julie told herself for the hundredth time as Monday afternoon dragged on. But in truth she could think of little else. She couldn't remember the last time she'd gotten so wrapped up in a guy. She was smart to cut it off now.

Smart, but not particularly happy.

With a sigh, she tried to focus on the spreadsheet on her computer. She was supposed to be going over the final arrangements for the cook-off, not mooning over one of their celebrities.

A knock came at the door of her office, and she looked up to see her mother in the doorway. Alicia Michaels gave her a tentative smile as she jumped to her feet.

"Mom, what are you doing here?" she asked in surprise.

"I was in the city, and I wanted to talk to you. I thought you might be able to get off work a little early and get a drink with me. Maybe one of those wine bars that are so popular now."

There was absolutely nothing about her mother's reply that made sense. Her mom rarely came to the city, never dropped by her office, and didn't drink anything stronger than diet coke. "What's wrong?"

Her mom fidgeted with the strap on her bag. "Nothing is wrong. I just want to talk to you. I mentioned that yesterday."

"You also said we could do it next weekend."

"Well, I can't wait that long. Can you get away for a bit?"

It was almost five, so she gave a nod. "Sure. There's a coffee place down the street. We can go there."

"Good," her mom said with relief. "That's perfect."

Julie grabbed her purse and ushered her mom out of the office, pausing a moment at the reception desk to say she'd be back in about an hour if anyone was looking for her.

"Do you really have to go back to work?" Alicia asked as they walked out of the building. "Isn't the day over?"

"There's a lot going on. My days rarely end at five."

"You work too hard, Julie."

"Everyone works hard. We're a non-profit. We run lean so the money can go to where it helps the most."

"Maybe you should consider getting out of non-profit and working on the corporate side of fundraising. I'm sure you've made a lot of connections."

"I'm not interested in that."

"It would pay you more money."

"What's going on, Mom?"

"Nothing. Can't a mother be worried about her daughter's financial future?"

She frowned but decided not to press her mother for more information until they had coffee and a table between them. Kat's Koffee House was warm and cozy with delicious coffee and even better pastries. After picking up their coffees, they sat down at a table by the window, sipping on skinny vanilla lattes.

Her mom looked tired, Julie thought. Her blue eyes were full of shadows and the lines across her forehead and around her mouth seemed more pronounced. The gray was beginning to show in the roots of her hair, and she'd lost weight, too. This was not the woman who'd gotten married with joy and exuberance three months earlier. "Okay," she said decisively. "You have to tell me what's wrong. You're starting to worry me. Is it Kent? Is it the marriage?"

"No, this has nothing to do with him. Well, maybe it has a little do with him, but he's not the reason I haven't been sleeping well the last few weeks." Her mother set down her coffee and twisted her hands together. "A long time ago, I made a decision out of anger. I knew it was wrong, but I did it anyway. I should have made it right years ago, but I didn't."

"What on earth are you talking about?"

"Your father."

She stiffened. "We don't talk about him, remember?"

Alicia nodded. "I know that was my rule. It was easier if I could just pretend he didn't exist. But that wasn't fair to you. I want to apologize Julie."

"You don't have anything to apologize for, and I don't even understand why we're talking about him now."

"You know that Kent has helped me deal with my bitterness and anger?"

"Yes," she said warily.

"Well, I confided in him, and he told me that I was never going to be free of the past until I came clean."

Her brows drew together. She couldn't make sense of what her mother was saying. "I don't understand."

Her mother stared back at her. "I know you don't, but you will." She reached into her bag and pulled out a large, thick manila envelope. "After your dad left, he sent you a letter. I don't know if you remember that, but—"

"I remember. I didn't want to read it."

"You gave it to me and told me to throw it away, but I just put it in my drawer. When other notes came in, I put them in the same place. I was angry. You were angry. We were both upset all the time. I thought I was doing the right thing. Or maybe that's not even true. I was just locking him in the drawer so I wouldn't have to think about him. He tried to call you a few times, but I intercepted the calls. I wouldn't give him your cell phone number, and I told him you'd be in touch when you were ready." Alicia gave her an apologetic look. "I realize now that I never wanted you to be ready, Julie. I didn't want to lose you to him. I was selfish. I wanted you on my side, and I was afraid that your dad might charm you into being on his side. So I deliberately did everything I could to keep you apart."

"After what he did to you, to our family, how could you think I would take his side?" she asked. "That wouldn't have happened in a million years."

"Maybe not, but I should have given you the chance to make that decision. So I'm giving you everything that he sent you over the years, and you can do whatever you want with the information."

She stared at the envelope like it was a snake about to bite. "I don't want it."

"I think you should look through his letters."

She shook her head, meeting her mom's gaze. "Why? I'm sure they're filled with meaningless apologies. Nothing he could say would change what he did to us."

Her mom let out a sigh. "He did it to me, Julie. He cheated on me. I was his wife. The other women had nothing to do with you and everything to do with me. Your father loved you very much. I thought I was punishing him by making it hard for him to get in touch with you, but I was punishing you, too, and it's taken me ten years to realize that."

"Dad could have found me after I left the house. He could have contacted me at college. I've been on my own for years. It's not that difficult to find someone on the Internet, so if he wanted to get in touch with me, he could have found a way."

"I'm sure he thinks you hate him. I told him that every time he called." Her mother blew out a breath. "I was such a basket case when he left. I don't know how I lost myself, but I did. I built my whole life around your dad. I was so in love with him. But the whole time we were together I was so worried about him cheating or walking away that I actually pushed him in that direction. He used to tell me that I was always testing him. I didn't know what he meant at the time, but I think now that I do know. I was jealous and clingy and questioning him over everything he did. I'd go through his phone. I'd read his email. I'd ask the other wives to ask their husbands what he was doing on the road. The older I got, the longer we were together, the more worried I became that I wasn't going to be enough for him. Beautiful women were always around your father. I felt like a middle-aged hag. Then the worst came true."

"You're not trying to say now that somehow Dad's cheating was your fault, are you?"

"No," her mom said quickly. "Definitely not. That's on him. I'm just saying that there was another side that you probably never heard or even saw, because I didn't want you to hear it or see it. When your father left, you were all I had left, and I became obsessed with keeping you away from him and making you feel the same way I felt. But that was wrong. I'm sorry, honey. I wish I could change it, but I can't. I can only try to do better now."

Julie sat back in her chair, her mind spinning from her mother's rapid-fire confession. "I don't know what to say."

"You don't have to say anything. I just needed you to hear me."

"It's so weird," she muttered. "How Dad's name keeps coming up all of a sudden. I didn't think about him for years, but the past week it has all come back."

Now it was her mother's turn to look confused. "This past week? But I just brought him up yesterday on the phone."

"Yes, but he came up in a bigger way for me when I had to go to the ballpark to invite a baseball player to participate in our Celebrity Cook-Off."

"You went to the Cougars' ballpark?" her mother asked in astonishment. "I'm surprised you didn't get someone else to do that."

"I tried, but everyone felt that with my last name I had a better shot at getting Matt Kingsley on board."

"Matt Kingsley," her mom echoed. "I remember him. He was one of the young guys your father mentored his last year or so in the game."

"Yeah, Matt has a great opinion of Dad. He thinks he's a hero."

"A lot of people felt that way about your father."

"Anyway, Matt asked me about Dad, and I found myself telling him the story, which, of course, made me think about everything that happened." She paused. "I really thought I knew the way it went down, but I must admit you're making me question a few things now."

"I'm trying to be as honest as I can be," her mom said. "Even though I'm terrified you're now going to hate me and want to go see him."

She reached across the table and put her hand over her mother's. "You don't ever have to worry about losing me, Mom."

"Even now that you know what I did?"

"I told you to put that first letter away."

"But you didn't know about the rest."

"I probably would have had the same reaction."

"Maybe not if you'd read one."

"Did you read them?"

"No, they're sealed, but I know how good your father is with words. He used to write me love letters when we were teenagers. I think I fell in love with him through those letters." Alicia drew in a big breath. "It feels good to get this out. It was weighing on me. I just hope by doing so, I'm not hurting you again."

"I'm fine. I'm all grown up now."

"I know. You're beautiful and smart, and I am so proud of you."

"Thanks."

Her mother pushed the envelope closer to her. "You really do need to keep this, Julie. If you want to throw the letters away, that's up to you, but I need to give them to you. I need to move on completely. Maybe I'm being selfish again—"

"You're not. You should move on."

"You should, too."

"Well, I went to the ballpark, didn't I?"

"You did do that." Her mom tilted her head. "As I recall Matt Kingsley was a very good-looking young man."

"He still is," she admitted.

"And he's single?"

"Yep. But I'm not going to go down that road."

Her mom gave her a helpless smile. "I'd certainly advise you not to, but it's your decision."

"I've decided not to see Matt again—well, except for the cook-off."

"It sounds like you've already seen him more than just once."

"I have. He's very charming, but you don't have to worry, Mom. I know exactly what I'm doing."

Her mother laughed and shook her head. "Oh, Julie. That's the exact same thing I said to your grandmother right before I married your father."

"It's not the same."

"Of course it's not. But I still need to tell you to be careful."

"Some people think I'm too careful," she murmured.

"Is one of those people Matt?"

She nodded. "Yes."

But it wasn't just Matt who thought she was too careful, she'd been thinking the same thing about herself. She wanted to protect her heart from more pain, but she also wanted to live her life with some passion. She just didn't know how to do both.

Chapter Eight

Being careful probably didn't include going to the Cougars stadium on Wednesday afternoon with a reporter who wanted to interview Matt. Julie had managed to book the interview through text and emails, but Matt had told her he wouldn't do the piece at all if she didn't come along. So here she was—standing in the first row of seats watching Matt take batting practice while she waited for the reporter to show up.

Being in the ballpark during practice was unsettling on a lot of levels. The memories of the days she'd spent watching her dad step into the batter's box washed over her. When she was a little girl, she'd often gone to the park with him before a game. Back then she'd loved the sport. She'd enjoyed watching the hitters, tracking the game, studying batting averages and reading scouting reports. In fact, those were the times where she'd felt the closest to her dad.

It had really been just the two of them on those occasions. When she was in middle school, she'd gone to almost every home game. She'd tag along with her dad to the ballpark to watch practice. Sitting in the stands those sunny afternoons, the smells of hot dogs, garlic fries and peanuts wafting in the air, had been really, really fun.

Her mother had never loved coming to the ballpark or

studying the intricacies of the sport. It was just what her husband did—not what he loved, or what she loved.

Funny, Julie hadn't realized that until just now.

Memories of being at the ballpark with her father coupled with what her mother had told her on Monday night, not to mention the unopened envelope that still sat on her coffee table, had her feeling completely off her game. It was as if time was spinning her around, showing her the past, then the present, even giving her a glimpse of the future, but it was all somehow tied to baseball.

She told herself to stay in the moment and stop getting so tied up in things that had happened years ago.

Focusing on Matt, she watched him hit for a good five minutes. He really was pretty amazing, she thought, helplessly drawn to everything about him. In the batter's box, he was aggressive and powerful. That was evident in his stance, in every swing of the bat. He also had a laser focus that allowed him to see the smallest movement of a baseball moving towards him at close to a hundred miles an hour.

He could adjust for the slower pitches, too, when the ball moved a lot slower, curving deceptively, starting out high and ending up at his ankles. Matt sent numerous balls soaring out to each field with line drives and hard-hit grounders mixed in with the occasional long ball to the fence.

Matt was one of the Cougars' top hitters, if not the top hitter, but more important than his overall average was his ability to hit in the clutch, when it counted, when it was two outs, bottom of the ninth, the game on the line. There was no one else the Cougars would rather have up than Matt Kingsley.

But Matt didn't seem as impressed with himself as the coaches surrounding the backstop behind the plate. He stopped to adjust his stance. He took off his helmet and wiped some sweat off his forehead and then took another swing. The ball dribbled toward the pitcher. Matt hit his bat on the ground and muttered something that sounded like a lot of swear words strung together. His coach came out and said something to him, and then he started hitting again.

She was beginning to see what he'd meant when he'd told her he had a hitch in his swing. It was an almost imperceptible lift of his right shoulder right before he struck the ball. She leaned forward, resting her arms on the rail in front of her as she focused on the movement of his body when his bat made contact with the ball. Pushing her sunglasses on top of her head, she gave herself a clearer line of vision. It was definitely there, she realized, noting when he hit a good ball and when he didn't.

Surely his coaches could see it. They were standing right behind him, although they didn't seem to be paying much attention now. They were talking to each other and one of them was motioning toward the dugout for the next hitter to step up.

"Julie Michaels?" a man said, interrupting her.

She turned her head to see a young man in his early thirties. "Yes?"

"I'm Dan Stern, SF Daily News."

"Of course." She shook his hand. "Mr. Kingsley is almost done, I think."

"Great."

"Can I give you any background information on the Celebrity Cook-Off while we wait for Mr. Kingsley to finish?"

"I've got all the details," Dan said, his attention on the field. "I've never been here unless there was an actual game going on. It's cool."

She inwardly sighed, having a feeling this interview was going to focus more on Matt and baseball than the fundraiser, but what could she do? She had to let it play out, and as long as the Foundation got a mention, it was better than nothing.

"I'm going to take a few shots of Matt hitting," Dan said, moving a few feet away to get a better view of Matt in the batter's box. Several moments later, he came back to join her. "He really drives the ball, doesn't he?"

"I guess that's why he's one of the best."

"How did you get him for your fundraiser?"

"I was very persuasive," she said, happy to see Matt making his way over to join them. As he came into the stands, he gave her a potent smile, his green eyes sparkling with pleasure. It was as if something secret, something intimate passed between them. Or maybe that was just her imagination.

She tried not to let her gaze or her smile linger. She was very aware of the nearby reporter, and the last thing she wanted was to start any rumors or distract the reporter from writing about the fundraiser. She introduced the two men and added a few sentences to start the conversation, then let Dan take over.

Matt handled the interview like the pro he was. He was friendly, concise and he made an effort to bring the interview back to the cook-off whenever Dan started getting too baseball-oriented in his questions. Twenty minutes later, a few more photographs taken, and the interview was wrapped. Dan told them he'd be in touch.

"That wasn't too painful," Matt said when they were alone.

"You made it easy. You knew exactly what he wanted, what I wanted, and you gave it to him."

"It's nice to know I can give you what you want some of the time."

"I do appreciate what you're doing for the Foundation."

"And I'm glad about that, but we both know that I'm doing a lot of it for you."

Goosebumps ran down her arms at the purposeful look in his eyes. "Well, whatever your reason, I'm grateful."

"Good. That should make my next question easier."

"What's your next question?" she asked warily.

"I want to take you to dinner."

"It's only four-thirty."

"Well, I didn't mean we were going to eat right this second. The place I have in mind is a bit of a drive. But I think you'll like it."

"There are a lot of restaurants about five minutes away," she said, feeling more than a little tempted to say yes to his invitation despite her intention to stay away from him. On the other hand, going back to work didn't really appeal, nor did going home hold much interest, because then she'd be faced with that unopened envelope filled with her father's letters.

"Just say yes," Matt told her.

She stared back at him. "Okay, yes."

He smiled with satisfaction. "Great. I'm going to change. I'll meet you by the car in twenty minutes?"

"All right."

He paused. "Don't change your mind, Julie."

"I won't. Like you, Matt, if I say I'm going to do something, I do it."

"Good."

As Matt left, an older man walked toward her. She knew that weathered, lined face and those cheerful brown eyes. They belonged to Dale Howard, the General Manager of the Cougars and one of her father's best friends.

"Is it you, Julie?"

She blew out a breath. "Mr. Howard."

"Oh come on now, call me Dale. You're all grown up."

"I am."

"It's great to see you. You're working with the charity Matt is supporting this month?"

She nodded. "We just finished an interview."

"I saw that. I couldn't believe it was you."

The last thing she wanted to do was talk to Dale, but she was a grown-up now, as he'd just reminded her, and she had to stop running away from things and people that reminded her of the past. "It's me."

"I want to apologize. I saw your name on my callback list a few days ago, but I had to go out of town. My daughter just had a baby."

She remembered Lucy Howard. They'd hung out together when they were twelve and thirteen. "Is it her first child?"

"Second. She got married right out of college. They live in Maine. She and her husband run an Inn up there."

"That sounds like a lovely life."

"It's a beautiful place, a long way from here though. Molly and I miss her all the time," he added, referring to his wife. "How's your mother?"

"She's good. She got remarried a few months ago."

"Well, that is excellent news. I know she had a hard time with things." His smile faded. "I didn't want to take sides, but your mom wouldn't talk to any of us once she and Jack split up. It was sad. I felt bad for her and for you."

"It was a long time ago," she said, starting to actually feel like it was a long time ago. Even though the past had popped back up in full glory in the past week, revisiting it had somehow made it seem less dramatic and painful than she'd thought. Or maybe it was just that she was starting to remember some of the good moments, too.

"So you're working in San Francisco now?"

"Yes, and I love what I do."

"Well, I know I wasn't responsive before, but if you need anything in the future, you let me know, and I'll try to help you out if I can," he said.

"That's great. We fund a lot of good causes. Your support would always make a difference. In fact, we still have some tickets left for the Celebrity Cook-Off. Wouldn't you like to see Matt in action in the kitchen?"

Dale laughed. "Now that does sound too good to pass up. Can you leave the details with my assistant?"

"Absolutely. Maybe you can bring Molly."

"She'll love it. She's a big fan of those cooking shows on television. And now that it's just the two of us, she's always trying out crazy recipes on me."

Dale's words reminded her that he'd managed to stay married to his wife for at least thirty years, and he'd been a player before moving into management some twenty years ago. Then again, there was always an exception to prove every rule.

"You speak to your dad at all?" Dale asked, a cautious note in his voice.

"No, I don't," she said honestly.

"I know he'd like to hear from you."

"Well, there was a time I would have liked to hear from him," she returned.

"I know he hurt you and your mom. He made some big mistakes."

"I don’t really want to talk about him."

"I understand. Well, if it won't bother your mother to hear my name, tell her that Molly and I think of her often."

"I will," she promised, thinking that her mother might actually be okay with hearing about Molly and Dale now. Since she'd found love again and had her own personal psychologist helping her to rebuild her life, she'd definitely changed and softened. It was as if love had chipped away at the wall of hate her mother had built up.

Had she built the same wall?

She had a feeling the answer was yes.

After saying goodbye to Dale, she walked out to the parking lot and waited for Matt. As usual, there were groupies around the player's entrance, but she knew now that Matt had another way out and eventually he would make his way to his car. She'd parked a few spots away, so she leaned against her car and waited. As she did so, she sent an email to Dale's assistant with the ticket information for the cook-off. He might have just been trying to be nice, but every ticket sale counted.

She had just sent the email when Matt walked out to join her. He'd obviously taken a quick shower. His brown hair was still damp, and his face was cleanly shaven. There was a nice musky scent clinging to him, too, which only made him that much more irresistible. He stopped in front of her. "We can take my car and get yours on the way back."

"They won't close the parking lot?"

"No, it will be fine."

"Okay."

She followed him to his car and slid into the passenger seat. Matt tossed a duffel bag in the back and then got behind the wheel.

"I saw Dale Howard heading your way," Matt said as he started the car. "How was that conversation?"

"It was fine. I'm sure you know that he and my father were good friends. Our families did a lot together when I was younger. I was pretty good friends with his daughter Lucy, too. I guess she just had a baby. Time really flies. Last time I saw her she was about fifteen. Now she is married with children."

"Lucy is a great girl. Her father is also a good guy, and he has an astute eye for talent."

"Because he picked you?"

He gave her a grin. "Well, that was one of his best moves." He paused, concentrating on merging onto the freeway for a moment. "Was it hard for you to be in the stadium?"

"I thought it would be more difficult than it turned out to be," she admitted.

"That's the thing about fear. Sometimes the monsters disappear when you look at them."

"Is that why you wanted me to be at the interview?"

"Actually, I just wanted to see you again."

She had a feeling his reason was more complicated than that, but she let it go.

"When's the last time you were at a game?" he asked.

"At least ten years. The new stadium is a lot nicer than the old one. The seats are closer to the action."

"And there's nowhere near as much wind. The organization and the city did a great job getting us a new home."

"Have you ever considered playing for another team?"

"Every time I come up for contract, I know I can be traded away, but I've been lucky that the Cougars have wanted to keep me and to pay me well. Some of my friends have bounced around from team to team for years. That's hard on the families."

"My father played for four teams during his career. I think that was part of the problem. My mom didn't want to take me out of school, so we never moved with him. We'd sometimes go to join him in the summer, but even those periods seemed to get shorter as I got older."

"The job can be hard on the family," Matt said. "But there are usually some perks to ease the pain."

"Would you go to another team if the Cougars didn't want to renew your contract?"

"Of course. I'd go anywhere I needed to go to keep playing. This is my career. And I'm going to play it as long as I can." He gave her a quick look. "Probably not what you wanted to hear."

She shrugged. "I was pretty sure of your answer when I asked the question. So are you going to tell me where we're going?"

"Palo Alto. I hope you don't mind if I take care of some of my own family business before we go to dinner."

"What kind of family business?"

"My youngest brother David goes to Stanford."

"He's the one who's thinking of dropping out?"

"Yes—dropping out of one of the best schools in the country that many people would kill to go to," Matt said with anger in his voice. "He's been avoiding my calls, but I happen to know where he'll be in about thirty minutes from now, so I'm going to ambush him."

"Do you really want me around for that?" she asked doubtfully.

"It won't take long. I'm sure David will try to blow me off after about five minutes, but I still have to try. I'd at least like him to finish out the year and not drop out now."

"That makes sense. But it sounds like your brother wants something that college can't give him."

"Yeah, he wants to be a rock star. I'm thinking maybe you can relate to that."

"Oh," she said, now understanding why he wanted her along. "Because I wanted to be in an orchestra once, you think David will relate to me in some way."

"It did occur to me," Matt admitted.

"He won't. In fact, I'm sure he'll think I sold out my passion for money. Not that I make a lot of money in a non-profit, but it's still a steady job with an income. And he wouldn't be wrong, Matt. There's a part of me that did give up on music because I was too afraid to live that kind of gypsy existence. I wanted to feel like I could take care of myself. So I'm not the right person to convince him to go for a business degree."

"Do you have regrets, Julie?"

"Not really. I like what I do now, so I'm okay with it. But that's just me. If your brother has a burning desire to be a musician, I don't think you'll be able to stop him."

"I'm fine with David playing music, but he has to have a day job, a way to support himself. I can't help him out forever. At some point, he has to be able to stand on his own feet, and I don't know that he can do that."

"Neither of you will probably know if he can do it, until he has to actually do it. It's like when the mama bird pushes the baby bird out of the nest when she thinks it's ready to fly. That's the real moment of truth. And most birds fly."

He smiled at her analogy. "Really? Do you actually know that?"

"Well, I don't have concrete proof, but there was a bird's nest in the backyard of the house I grew up in, and I never saw a dead baby bird on the sidewalk. And at some point, they all flew away."

"Well, I'm not David's mother, so I don't have the maternal instinct."

"That's true," she murmured. "Where is your mom in all this? Why doesn't she talk to David?"

"I haven't told her that he's thinking of dropping out."

"Has David told her?"

"I doubt it."

"Why not?"

Matt hesitated, then said, "I think my mom was so busy trying to keep things together that as kids we tried not to bother her with small problems. I used to tell everyone to come to me first. They got into that habit, and it stuck."

In a lot of ways Matt had become the father of the family, she realized. That had been a lot of responsibility to take on as a kid. "I can understand why you did what you did back then, but now you're working a lot, and I get the feeling your mom is not? Or is she?"

"She still works part time at a clothing boutique, but now it's because she likes it, not because she has to. I've made sure she'll be okay if she never wants to work again."

"Then maybe it's time to let her share in some of these issues with your siblings."

"I'm going to see if I can handle it," Matt said.

Of course he was going to do that. He was not a man to ask for help.

Silence fell between them as Matt maneuvered his way through a freeway interchange. Traffic was getting heavy with the evening commute, but Matt seemed to find open lanes whenever he could.

She hadn't been out of the city in a while, and it was nice to have a break. She loved San Francisco, but sometimes with the fog-enshrouded nights, her world started to feel a little small.

She'd grown up on the Peninsula, in a big house in Atherton, a city right next to Palo Alto. It was the one thing her mother hadn't lost in the divorce. However, after Julie went to college, her mom had sold the house and moved into a two-bedroom apartment. Now Julie couldn't help wondering if perhaps there had been an agreement for her mom to keep the house until she graduated from high school.

As they neared Palo Alto, she felt a wave of nostalgia for her hometown, an emotional connection that only increased when Matt drove down University Avenue toward Stanford.

"This street has changed a lot," she murmured. "New shops and restaurants. It's very trendy."

"It was always like this, wasn't it?"

"There used to be fewer chain stores and more small shops," she said. "I forgot you went to college here for a year."

"Yeah, but at the time, I wasn't old enough to explore the neighborhood bars, so I spent most of my time on campus or at the baseball stadium. But I did like living here. The university has so much to offer. I don't understand how David could want to leave."

"How old is David?"

"He just turned twenty, but he's acting like he's twelve."

"Well, I wouldn't tell him that," she said dryly.

"I'll try to refrain." He stopped at a red light and gave her a quick look. "So tell me something, Julie."

"What's that?"

"Did you miss me?"

"It's only been two days since I saw you."

"A long two days."

She'd like to think his comment came from the heart, but Matt's charm practically oozed out of his pores. "They flew by for me," she said, refusing to let herself get taken in by his smile.

"Ouch," he said. "You know how to hit where it hurts."

"I doubt I could hurt you, Matt."

"I think you underestimate yourself," he said, a quiet, reflective note in his voice now.

She didn't know what to say to that, so she said nothing.

A few moments later, Matt drove onto the campus and turned into a parking lot. The Stanford campus was beautiful and spacious with plenty of open land and beautiful oak trees. It was funny to think of Matt going to school here, being an eighteen-year-old kid, trying to make it as a college player, only to be launched into the big leagues before he was out of his teens. Which reminded her of what she'd noticed earlier.

"I wanted to tell you that I was watching you hit today, and I think I figured out the problem with your swing."

"Oh, yeah?" he said in surprise as he parked the car. "Coach said I looked fine."

"Then he wasn't watching very closely. Your right shoulder lifts just before you make contact. It's a very small movement. I think it has to do with your stride. When you lift your left leg, you're maybe a beat behind, and then the shoulder lifts to compensate. I noticed it more on the slider than anything else."

He turned off the engine. "You can recognize a slider?"

"I can recognize any pitch. I'll show you what I mean," she said, getting out of the car.

Matt joined her behind the car. She mimicked his stance and then tried to show him the way his shoulder lifted with his stride. "See?"

He gave her a look that told her she was out of her mind.

"What? You don't think I know what you're talking about?"

"For a woman who hates baseball as much as you do, you seem to think you know a lot about my hitting stance."

"I watched my dad hit baseballs for at least ten years. And he'd sit with me and we'd critique the other players after he was done hitting. I listened and I learned. Show me your stance and your stride."

"I'm not going to do that here."

"No one is around," she said, taking a quick look. The parking lot was empty. "Unless you're afraid I'm right, and you don't want to admit it."

"Okay, fine." He turned to the side and listed his hands as if he were holding a bat.

"Now show me your swing."

He strode forward and swung his hands in front of him.

She frowned. "Well, that looks good. I didn't see the hitch."

"That's because I was thinking about keeping my shoulder down." He paused and shook his head in bemusement. "I can't believe you saw that and no one else did. You must have been watching me pretty closely."

She cleared her throat as he moved towards her. "I didn't have anything else to do while I was waiting for the reporter."

"Or maybe you just couldn't take your eyes off of me," he said lightly, sliding his hands around her waist.

"Uh, I wouldn't say that."

"I would."

"What are you doing, Matt?"

"Thanking you for fixing my swing."

"You could just say thank you."

"I like to back up my words with actions." He lifted one hand and slid it through her hair, cupping the back of her head and then deliberately lowered his mouth to hers. "Thanks, Julie."

The kiss was way too short, and as he lifted his head, she had to fight the urge to throw her arms around his neck and pull his head back down for a second kiss and a third. But somehow she managed to control herself.

"You are becoming a really bad habit," she said with a sigh. "Why do you have to be such a good kisser?"

"I never thought it was a problem before," he said with a grin. "But it's not just me. We're good together. Let me show you."

"You already did," she said, putting a hand on his chest as he leaned in. "You need to focus on why we're here. Your brother, remember?"

"Right." He straightened as he checked his watch. "He should be just about done."

"With what?"

"He plays guitar at a campus coffeehouse three times a week from four to five-thirty," he said. "It's not too far from here."

She fell into step with him, happy to have the attention on Matt's family for a change. But from everything she'd heard about David, she had a feeling that David was more like Matt than Matt wanted to admit, which should make his upcoming ambush even more interesting.

Chapter Nine

The coffee house was packed with students. Almost every table was taken. While most university coffeehouses were filled with students working on laptops, leafing through textbooks, or engaging in conversation, this one was completely quiet, everyone's attention focused on the young man at the front of the room, who with his voice and guitar captivated the room.

They stood in the back as David sang in a low, melodic tone that was hypnotic and soothing and yet compelling, all at the same time. David was definitely a younger version of Matt. His brown hair was a bit darker and longer than Matt's and David had a scruffy beard across his cheeks. But when David looked out at the crowd, he had the same penetrating green eyes, the same intangible charisma. Two girls at the front table looked at David with complete adoration. She'd seen that same look on the faces of women who watched Matt. The Kingsley men certainly had a way with women.

"He's good," she whispered to Matt.

Matt's lips tightened at her words. "He can be good after he goes to class and does his homework."

"He's not a little kid anymore," she couldn't help reminding him.

"He is to me."

When David finished playing, the room burst into applause.

David thanked everyone for listening and then set his guitar down and stood up. Women instantly surrounded him. It was another twenty minutes before he made his way across the room. By that time, Matt was literally seething with impatience, but he'd decided not to confront David until he was done with his fans.

David stopped abruptly when he saw Matt. There was instant tension between them.

"We need to talk," Matt said firmly.

"You shouldn't have come down here," David replied. "I'm busy."

"Give me ten minutes. You owe me that."

David hesitated and a silent battle went on between the two men. Finally David nodded and waved them toward a newly abandoned table. Since David had finished playing, the room had cleared out.

"This is Julie," Matt said. "My brother David."

"I really enjoyed your playing," she said. "You're really good."

"Thanks." David let out a sigh as he faced his older brother. "Say what you have to say."

"Connor told me you want to drop out of school."

"I'm thinking about it."

"It's a bad idea, David. Being in college is just a few years out of your life, but they are years that are really hard to complete later on in life. You need to finish school now, before you have other responsibilities."

"You quit. You took a chance on the career you wanted," David reminded Matt.

"That was different. When I went pro, the Cougars agreed to pay all my college expenses if it didn't work out. If you leave, you have no backup. And I'm not going to support you unless you're in school."

"I can take care of myself," David replied. "No one

asked you to support me."

Matt gave him a look of incredulousness. "Are you serious? You've been asking me for stuff your entire life. The car you drive—that came from me. The guitar you just played was last year's Christmas present."

David frowned. "Well, if you want to count gifts…"

"I don't want to count anything. I want you to stay in school, get a degree, and then if you want to pursue music, fine."

"I don't see the point of wasting time in classes that aren't going to get me anywhere."

"You're getting an education and a degree. That's important."

"To you," David muttered.

"It will matter to you one day, too. At least promise me you'll finish out the year before you make any decisions."

David stared back at him. "All right. I'll finish out the year. But I don't know about next year. I have some opportunities in music I want to explore. And I think you would have turned pro even if you hadn't had backup," David added. "You love what you do. Don't you think I should be able to have the same feeling?"

"Of course. But you have to be practical, too. Music equipment, recording, costs money."

"I'm not an idiot, Matt. I am going to Stanford after all, and while you might pay my tuition, it was my grades that got me in here. Let's not forget that."

"I know you're a smart kid. I just don't know why you're acting so stupid right now."

Julie winced a little at Matt's sharp words, but David just laughed. "You only think I'm stupid because I don't agree with you. And if anyone is being stupid, it's Connor. Getting married after three months of dating someone he only sees like twice a week. Now that is crazy."

"I don't disagree. Did you tell him that?"

"Yeah, but he doesn't listen to me. You're the only one who has any influence over him."

"I doubt that. He laughed at me. He told me I didn't know what love was."

"Well, that's probably true. Look, I gotta go, Matt. I actually do have to work on a paper for school."

"Go," Matt said waving his hand in the air. "But promise me you will talk to me before you drop out of school or make any other big decisions."

"You'll be busy once the season starts."

"I can answer the phone. And if I'm tied up, I'll call you back.

David rolled his eyes. "Fine, but no one calls anymore. I'll text you if I need you." He looked at Julie. "Nice to meet you."

"You, too," she murmured. As David left, she said to Matt, "That seemed to go pretty well."

"Did it?" Matt sighed. "David tends to tell me what I want to hear and then does whatever the hell he wants."

She smiled at his irritated tone. "Stubborn independence seems to be a family trait. You just have to find a way to let go—like the mama bird."

"The problem isn't me kicking David out of the nest. He wants to fly; I just think he's going to fall on his face. He needs to be better prepared before he leaves school. He's being stupid. Don't you agree?"

"I honestly don't know. I think degrees are important. It's hard to get good jobs without one. On the other hand, your brother is really talented. I can see why he's torn."

"It's so impossibly difficult to make it in the music business."

"I'd say the odds are even bigger for someone to make it as a professional baseball player, so I don't think you can really talk to your brother about odds."

"I know. I'm not the best example for this situation. Maybe I'll call Claire and get her to talk to David. She might be able to get through to him."

"You're a good brother, Matt. One day I'm sure you'll be a good father and not just a surrogate father."

A strange look flitted through his eyes. "I don't know about that," he muttered.

"What do you mean?" she asked, surprised by his words.

"I don't know if I want to have kids."

"Really? But you're so connected to your family."

"Exactly. I'm too connected. In some ways, I already feel like I raised a family or that I'm still raising them, and I'm not doing that good of a job."

"But these are your siblings. Your kids would be yours. You'd be there from the beginning."

"I was there for the beginning of my siblings' lives," he argued.

"But you were a little kid. Connor is only three years younger. Of course he's not going to listen to you. And David and Claire see you as their brother, not their dad. They had a dad, apparently a really good one."

"He was good, but I told you that David doesn't even remember him. I try to keep him alive in everyone's memories, but as time goes on, it's not that easy."

She liked that he tried to keep his dad alive. And she liked how much he cared about his brothers and sister and mom. But she didn't really like the thought of him not wanting kids.

Not that it should matter to her. She wasn't going to be his wife. She wasn't going to have to worry about that decision. Still…

"Don't you think you'd miss out if you didn't have children of your own?" she asked.

"Like I said, I've done a lot of the parenting stuff." He paused. "It sounds like you really want kids, Julie."

"I do. I love children. And I was an only child, so I was always jealous of people who had big families. Not that I wasn't spoiled with attention from my mom, but it would have been nice to have a sibling, especially after my dad left. So, yes, I do want kids some day. I'm not in a hurry. But I work with a lot of kids, and I just know that at some point in my life, I'm going to want a family." She paused, thinking that their opposing feelings about kids were just another reason why she and Matt had no future together. That thought shouldn't have been as depressing as it was. "So what now?" she asked. "I think you promised me dinner somewhere."

"I did." He straightened in his chair, pulling himself out of the contemplative mood he'd sunk into. "But I have to confess something first."

"What's that?" she asked warily.

"David isn't the only one I'm ambushing tonight. My friend Gary and his wife invited us to dinner, and they live about fifteen minutes from here."

"You want me to go to dinner with your friends?"

"I had dinner with your friends."

"Then why be cagey about it? Wait. Gary—is that Gary Hartman, the Cougars' all-star centerfielder?"

"That would be the one," he admitted. "Gary and Connie have been friends of mine for a long time. I'd love for you to meet them, but there will be baseball talk. I could say there wouldn't be, but I'd be lying. With spring training starting in a week, it's going to come up. If you don't want to go, I will call them and beg off."

"That would be rude. You should have told me, Matt. You claim to be an honest person, but you didn't act that way tonight."

"I know. I just didn't want you to say no, and I figured once we got there—"

"I'd cave," she finished.

"I can drive you back to the city. It's not really that big of a deal. I'll see them another night."

"No, I'll go with you," she said. Getting involved with Matt's baseball life wasn't her first choice, but she could handle it, and deep down she was a little curious to meet his friends. "But you're going to owe me, Matt."

"I'm sure I will," he said with a grin. "Just let me know when you want to collect."

"I will definitely do that."

* * *

As Matt rang the bell at the Hartman's two-story house, Julie felt a little nervous, and she didn't really know why. It shouldn't matter what the Hartmans thought of her. She'd probably never see them again after tonight.

Matt gave her a smile and slipped his hands into hers, squeezing her fingers. "They're going to love you. And I think you'll enjoy them, too."

"Are you reading my mind?"

"Maybe just your tension."

The door opened, and Julie found herself looking at a petite busty woman with dark red hair that fell down to her waist and a pair of curious brown eyes. After introductions, Connie gave Matt a hug and then turned to Julie.

"It's so nice to meet you, Julie. Come in." She grabbed Julie's hand and pulled her into the house. "Gary is getting the barbecue going. Why don't you help him, Matt? Julie and I will get acquainted."

"Julie?" Matt questioned, a gleam of concern in his eyes.

"I'll be fine. I'm more worried about dinner if you're

going to be helping Gary cook," she said lightly.

Both Connie and Matt laughed. Connie looked at Matt. "I see she knows how good you are in the kitchen."

"Unfortunately, she does."

"Well, Gary can grill. What he can't seem to do is get the propane tank hooked up to the new barbecue."

"I'm on it," Matt said, as he headed down the hall.

"Let's go into the kitchen," Connie said. "I'll get you some wine, and you can tell me how you met Matt."

"As long as I get the wine first, I'm happy to answer questions."

"A girl after my own heart."

Connie led Julie into a beautiful gourmet kitchen.

"Wow, this is amazing," she said, looking around at the endless granite countertops and sparkling appliances.

"I designed it myself," Connie said proudly. "We've spent the last year redoing the house and we're finally done—just in time, too. Red or white wine?"

"Red is fine. In time for what?" she asked as Connie poured her a glass of wine.

Connie's eyes sparkled. "Well, I wasn't going to say anything until later, but I'm pregnant."

"That's wonderful. Congratulations."

"We're really excited. I'm not quite three months yet, and I shouldn't be shouting it to the rooftops, but I can't seem to stay quiet about it. Have a seat," she said, waving Julie toward one of the stools at the counter. "We can chat while I finish the salad. I have to tell you that I was really surprised when Matt told me he was bringing a woman to meet us. He hasn't introduced us to anyone in a couple of years. How did you two meet?"

"I work for the California Children's Foundation. I asked Matt to participate in our Celebrity Cook-Off next Sunday."

"So you're the one who got him to do that. Matt insisted

that Gary and I buy tickets. How could we resist? The idea of Matt cooking in front of a crowd is just too incredible to pass up." Connie paused. "But since I now know you know he can't cook, what on earth is he going to make?"

"I taught him how to make scallops and risotto. I think he can replicate it, but we'll see. The hotel banquet kitchen has the recipe, and they'll be providing the food for everyone but the contest judges, so at the very least Matt will not poison the entire room."

"Thank goodness for that," Connie said, as she sliced some tomatoes and threw them into a salad. "So are you two a couple?"

"I wouldn't say that. We're…" She actually did not know how to finish the sentence. "Friends," she finished somewhat weakly.

Connie shot her a look that told her she wasn't buying that for a second. "Matt said you were important."

"Really? That's the word he used."

"It is, and I think I was as shocked when I heard him say it as you are now. Do you feel the same way about him?"

"I honestly don't know how I feel about him. I don't know if Matt mentioned to you that I'm not exactly a baseball fan."

"He did. He told us that you're Jack Michaels' daughter, and we know that your father divorced your mother."

"He didn't just divorce her; he cheated on her."

"I'm sorry. I'd kill Gary if he did that to me."

"Do you worry about it?" Julie asked, genuinely curious. "There are a lot of women hanging around the ballpark."

"Sure there are," Connie said easily. "But I trust Gary. We've been together for ten years. I knew him when he was a nobody. We've grown up together."

"That probably helps," she said, sipping her wine. "You started out at the same place." Although, that hadn't helped her parents. They hadn't just grown up together; they'd also grown apart.

"It's harder for the guys who are already rich and famous to know who's being real with them," Connie said. "I know Matt has had a hard time with that."

"I'm not sure I'd call being surrounded by supermodels a hard time," she said dryly.

Connie grinned. "I like you, Julie. And I'm starting to see why Matt likes you, too. You're not overly impressed with his celebrity. That's a change for him."

"He takes it as a challenge. He's determined to make me change my mind about baseball players."

"That sounds like it could be fun. There's nothing like a man determined to show you a good time. I hope you make him work for it."

Julie smiled. "And now I'm beginning to see why Matt likes you so much. Tell me how you and Gary met."

"I was his chemistry tutor in college. Eventually, I started tutoring him in other things—like how to treat a woman. He was a very good student. He got an A in chemistry and an A with me. We started going out, and we were pretty much inseparable after that. I was with Gary when he got drafted and through the first three years in the minors where he was continually being moved from team to team. There was a time there when neither one of us was sure he was going to make it, but eventually the Cougars called him up, and he's been there the last seven years. Baseball has been good to us. I don't know how long that will last, but we try to stay in the moment. That's all anyone can do right? None of us can predict the future."

"That's true," she said slowly, wondering if living in the moment was something common to ballplayers. Maybe knowing their careers would be short made every day more important.

"Can I top off your wine?" Connie inquired, reaching for the bottle on the counter.

Julie shook her head. She needed to keep her wits about her. She was already feeling much too comfortable in the cozy kitchen.

The outside door suddenly burst open, and Matt ran into the room with a huge grin on his face.

Gary had obviously imparted the good news.

Matt reached for Connie and gave her a hug. "Congratulations! I can't believe it. This time next year there will be little Hartmans running around."

"Make that little Hartman, singular, please," Connie commanded, extricating herself from Matt's arms with a laugh.

"I can't believe it," Matt continued. "You two are going to be parents. Your life is definitely going to change."

"In a good way," Connie said.

"Sure, if you consider getting up three times a night and changing diapers a good time," Gary teased.

She playfully slugged her husband in the arm. "You'll love every minute of it. And I don't think you've said hello to Julie yet."

Gary gave her a sheepish smile as he came over to say hello. "I am sorry about that. Matt was helping me get the barbecue going and then I had to tell him the big news. Happy you could join us tonight, Julie."

"Me, too, and congratulations."

"Thanks. Are the steaks ready for the grill?" he asked Connie.

She tipped her head toward the platter on the counter. "They're all yours. I need to run upstairs for a minute. I'll be right back."

As Gary took the steaks out to the grill, Matt came over to Julie. "Sorry to desert you like that."

"I'm a big girl. I can take care of myself. I like your friends."

Matt perched on the stool next to hers. "I'm really glad about that." He rested his hands on her thighs. "You're becoming very important to me, Julie." His green eyes darkened with emotion. "I want you to know that."

"I feel the same way," she said softly, her nerves tingling as he repeated what Connie had already told her. "I don't really want to, you know?"

His mouth spread into a slow smile. "I know. Don't fight it, sweetheart."

"That's not very good advice. I should fight it. You should, too. We're really different people, Matt. Baseball aside, we don't want the same things."

"The only thing I want right now is another kiss."

"Gary and Connie could come back at any second," she protested.

"Then we better do this fast."

He cupped her face with his hands. His kiss was warm, tender, promising. Her lips parted and she swiped her tongue across his lips.

Matt groaned and pulled her closer, prolonging the kiss until they were breathless. Shaken by the explosive passion of what was meant to be a lighthearted kiss, they simply stared at each other for a long moment, and then Matt blew out a breath. "I would love to get you out of here and finish what we just started."

"We can't leave. We haven't had dinner yet." And she could not finish what they'd just started, so maybe that was a good thing.

"You're right." Matt stood up. He extended his hand and pulled her to her feet. "Let's help Gary with the barbecue. We both need some air."

She wished that was all she needed.

Chapter Ten

The rest of the evening passed in a blur of conversation and laughter. Matt and Gary had first met in the minors, and they had hundreds of stories to tell about their experiences back then and another hundred to tell about their recent years with the Cougars. They were roommates on the road, so they were about as close as any two players could be. Once in a while, Matt offered her an apologetic glance and tried to steer the conversation away from baseball, but within minutes they would be right back where they started.

Julie was surprisingly interested and entertained by their stories. While some of their experiences brought back memories from her past, they didn't sting as much as they used to. And it was different to hear about baseball as an adult and not as a kid. She had a different perspective now.

She also liked how humble both Matt and Gary were. They really didn't take their talent or their good fortune for granted. They knew they were only as good as their last game and that every at bat was the start of something new. They were both really good and could certainly live off some glory days, but they didn't. They also had a genuine love of the game, which reminded her of her father, because he had loved baseball with all of his heart. She couldn't really blame him for that—just for everything else.

Her father had gotten caught up in his fame. He'd started to believe the world should revolve around him. She didn't get the same vibe from Matt or from Gary. In fact, watching Gary and Connie together, she saw an equal relationship, a loving, teasing partnership, and it was clear that they were madly in love with each other. She suspected that was partly why Matt had brought her to dinner. He wanted her to see a baseball relationship that was good and that was working.

Finally calling the evening to an end just before ten, they said their goodbyes, got in the car and headed back to San Francisco.

"Well?" Matt asked about ten minutes into their quiet drive.

She gave him a smile. "It was fun. Connie and Gary are great. They're down-to-earth, really good people."

Her words put a smile on his face. "I thought you'd like them. I can't believe they're going to have a kid. This time next year there will be a baby." He shook his head in bemusement. "Gary acts more like a kid than an adult most of the time."

"Then he'll be able to relate to his child really well. It will be more difficult for Connie. She'll be the one holding things together while Gary is playing."

"I know it can be hard on the wives," Matt admitted. "But the Cougars are a family team. They try to offer as much help as they can to the families. I know a lot of the women are friends and support each other."

"Connie mentioned that. She said some of them play softball together in the off-season and make the guys watch the kids."

"I forgot about that." He gave her a quick, curious look. "Did you ever play?"

"Yes, of course. I was my father's daughter, after all. I started when I was about seven and played until I was thirteen. I was good, too."

"What position did you play?"

"Early on I was a pitcher, because no one else could actually get the ball near the plate, and my father was a pitcher, so I thought it was cool to have his position. But I didn't really like that fast pitch motion. It hurt my arm. So I moved over to shortstop."

He turned and met her gaze. "My position?"

"Well, you're not the only shortstop in the world," she said with a laugh. "I was good at grounders, and I could throw pretty hard. My dad had made sure that I did not throw like a girl."

"He must have been proud of you."

"He hardly ever made it to a game. Maybe a half-dozen times in all those years."

"Sorry."

She shrugged. "It was just the way it was. I didn't hold it against him back then. I accepted his life; it was the only life I'd ever known. I respected that he was doing his job. But later, after everything went to hell, I realized that he hadn't always been working when he was away from home. Sometimes he was on a week-long fishing trip or hiking in the mountains or biking to Mexico with his friends. He was a very active man. And the off-season got shorter and shorter. He would head to spring training weeks before it actually started. I guess those were all signs of his discontent and trouble in the marriage, but I was a kid, so I didn't know. I didn't pick up on the signals."

"Your mother should have?"

"Well, they did fight a lot, so I guess she suspected something was wrong." She drew in a breath and let it out. "Anyway, it was all a long time ago. I haven't thought this much about those days in a very long time, but meeting you brought it all back."

"Sorry about that."

She shrugged. "It's not your fault."

"I'm glad you've finally admitted that."

She ignored his comment. "Don't forget we need to stop at the ballpark so I can get my car."

"I haven't forgotten."

A few minutes later, he turned into the empty stadium lot and parked next to her car. She stepped onto the pavement and shivered as a cold breeze from the bay lifted the air off of her neck.

Matt met her by her car as she dug into her bag for her keys.

"It's a beautiful night," he said.

"Cold, but pretty," she agreed, looking out at the bay and the sky. "No fog tonight, just a lot of stars."

"Yeah," he said, lifting his face toward the sky. "Did I ever tell you that at one point in my life I wanted to be an astronomer?"

"No. Seriously?"

"Yes. My dad loved looking into the sky. He had a telescope that he put up on the roof of our house, and he used to take me up there and tell me where the different stars were. I loved the idea of being part of a bigger universe."

"You should hang out with Alex Donovan then. He has an incredibly high-powered telescope on the roof of his office building. He and Andrea took me up there one night and it was amazing. I felt like I was actually in space."

"He did mention that to me once. I'll have to take him up on his offer to try it out. We should go out with them sometime. I'd like to meet Andrea."

His words made her feel like they were a couple, which was both exciting and terrifying. She really needed to figure out what she wanted from Matt.

"Don't you think that would be fun?" he prodded.

"Sure. But your life is going to get busy in another week. You'll be gone and on the road. Who knows when we could make that happen?"

"That's all true, but I try to make time for what's important—who's important," he said, putting his arms around her.

"Really?" she asked doubtfully.

"You don't believe me?"

"I think you believe what you're saying; I just don't know if you aren't being overly optimistic."

He smiled. "Well, a pessimist like you would think that."

"I'm really not that negative," she protested.

"With me, you are."

"Because I just don't see where this can go."

"You don't have to see the future now. You just have to feel good about this moment."

He pulled her into his arms and gave her a long hug. She slid her arms around his waist and rested her head on his shoulder, and felt incredibly warm and safe and protected in the circle of his embrace. They clung together for several minutes, just enjoying the feel of each other's bodies, but the sense of comfort gradually slipped away, replaced by a nervous tingling, and a needy desire, a hunger for more.

She lifted her head. Matt gazed down at her with intensity in his green eyes, and her heart leapt against her chest, beating wildly as anticipation built within her.

"Kiss me already," she whispered.

He smiled. "I thought you'd never ask."

She put her arms around his neck and pulled his head down to hers.

Every time her mouth met his, she felt her heart swell with emotion. Kissing Matt was starting to feel like going home or going to that perfect happy place, that incredible moment where everything was right with the world. She didn't want the connection to end. She wanted to stay like this forever.

But she couldn't do that. It had to end at some point, didn't it?

She hated when the voice of reason was able to battle past her emotional and physical response to Matt, but there it was again. She couldn't seem to turn off her finely tuned sense of caution.

She broke the kiss and pulled away. "I should go. I have to get to work early tomorrow."

"It's getting harder to say goodnight to you, Julie."

Her pulse jumped again at his words. She had a feeling that most women would have been in bed with Matt by now.

The image of them in bed together only made her more tense.

She licked her lips, not sure what to say.

Matt jumped into the breach. "Can we get together tomorrow night?"

She really, really wanted to. "I can't."

"Why not?" he demanded.

"I have a work commitment. And we just spent the evening together. This is moving a little too fast, Matt."

"I want to spend as much time as possible with you before I leave for spring training."

She was both touched and troubled by his words. She wanted to spend time with him, too. But she was starting to like him too much. How was she going to feel when he left? She'd been guarding her heart for a very long time, and that voice in her head was screaming at her to be careful because Matt could really hurt her—if she let him.

He put his hands on her shoulders, his fingers kneading the tight muscles. "Relax, Julie. You don't have to make any big decisions now. We're just getting to know each other. I'll meet you tomorrow after your work thing."

"It will be late," she said, his hands feeling a little too good, his smile way too irresistible.

"I don't care how late it is."

"Well, if you really want to spend time with me tomorrow, then you can help me with my work project."

"What does that involve?"

"Why don't I surprise you?" she said. "In fact, consider it a collection of your debt."

His smile broadened. "All right, it's a deal."

"Come by my office at six."

"I'll be there."

He gave her a quick kiss and then opened her car door.

She got inside and started the engine. As she drove home, his headlights followed her all the way back to her apartment. She could still invite him in…

But as she turned into her driveway, Matt waved goodbye and sped off into the night.

One less decision to make.

* * *

Matt didn't know what he was getting into when he arrived at Julie's office Thursday evening, but as long as he was spending time with her, he didn't really care. He couldn't seem to get her out of his head, and he was beginning to worry about that. But he wasn't going to think about the future right this second. He just wanted to spend time with her, see where things went…

When he entered her office, he heard voices and laughter and followed the noise to a large, brightly lit conference room where Julie and a half-dozen teenagers were surrounded by what he could only describe as a lot of crap: colorful bags, ribbons, t-shirts, hats, buttons and other stuff.

Julie looked up and saw him standing in the doorway. He liked the way she immediately smiled at him, the way her lips parted so invitingly as if she couldn't wait to kiss him again.

"Matt," she said, giving him a wave. "Come on in. I want you to meet everyone."

All eyes in the room turned on him, some gazes filling with instant recognition. There were four girls and three boys, all of whom appeared to be between the ages of thirteen and fifteen. They were a mixed group of Caucasian, Hispanic, Asian and African American.

"This is Matt Kingsley, the All-Star Shortstop for the Cougars," she said. "Meet Maya, Kevin, Latasha, Kristina, Ben, Luka and Hannah. They're the swag crew for the Celebrity Cook-Off."

"Swag, of course," he said, beginning to understand what he'd volunteered for.

"We're putting bags together for each one of the two-hundred and fifty guests."

"Great," he muttered, thinking that meeting Julie for a drink later would have been a much better idea.

She smiled. "I thought you'd enjoy it."

"What can I do?"

"We were just discussing the most efficient way to do this," Julie answered. "Ben suggested an assembly line."

"Or two," the girl named Maya put in. "We can do each side of the table."

"Good idea," Julie said. "Why don't you guys start setting it up? We'll put the bags first and then some of the bigger, more solid items next, followed by the smaller gifts." After delivering that instruction, she walked around the table to Matt and gave him a pointed look. "Last chance to bail."

He could see the challenge in her eyes. She kind of

wanted him to bail, but he wasn't going to give her the satisfaction. "Are you kidding? I'm excited to lend a hand."

"Okay, then let's get started. Hopefully, with all hands on deck, this shouldn't take too long."

"Who can I help?" Matt asked.

All of the kids answered at once. "Why don't I start with the bags?" he suggested. "I'm not that good at making anything look pretty." He took a position next to Maya, who seemed to be the natural leader of the group.

"I will be right back," Julie said. "I have to get a few things from my office."

As Julie left, Maya started giving orders, the first one to him. "If you want to just get the bags out of the boxes and then pass them to me, I'll take it from there."

"Sounds like a plan."

"I saw you play last year," Ben interjected, as he began the same operation on the other side of the table. "You made three double plays in one game. It was cool."

"That must have been against the Cubs," he said. "One of my best games."

"I'm going to play shortstop and second base this year on my school team," Kevin put in. "Maybe you could give me some tips."

"First tip is always watch the ball," he said. "It doesn't matter whether you're fielding or hitting, your eye has to be on that ball, and you have to want that ball to come to you. If you don't, you'll always be a split second behind."

"What's another tip?" Ben asked.

"Don't overthink," he said. "Baseball can be pretty simple, but when you get into your head it gets more difficult. You can't let what happened at the last at bat affect the next one. You're always starting over."

"I think baseball is boring," Hannah declared. "But the players are cute." She gave him a teenaged smile that he was sure would break a million hearts over the next few years.

"So do you guys all go to school together?" he asked.

"Some of us do," Latasha said. "But we all see each other at Baycrest. It's an afterschool program for kids that don't have anywhere else to go."

"The Foundation gives Baycrest money," Maya said. "Otherwise, they'd have to shut down."

"And we wouldn't be able to use their computers or get help on our homework or just have a safe place to go," Kristina said, speaking for the first time.

"It sounds like a good place," he said, making a mental note to see what else he could do to help their program.

"How's it going?" Julie asked, returning to the room.

"Good," he said.

She nodded approvingly. "Then I'm going to leave you all to do this while I finish up some other work."

"Hey, I thought we were spending time together," he said quietly as she moved past him.

"We will, but work comes first. Surely, you understand that better than anyone."

He nodded. "I do. I'll see you later then."

For the next hour and a half, he and the kids packed the bags of swag and set them into large boxes on the floor that would later be transported to the cook-off. Matt was actually impressed with the willingness of the teens to work so hard. For the most part, they stayed pretty focused, although they did have a lot of questions for him, especially the boys. But he didn't mind. Talking to them made the time pass that much faster.

As he caught a glimpse at just how much work went into the fundraisers from behind the scenes, he became more impressed with Julie's job. He was always the one on the stage or at the podium or giving a press interview. But these kids and Julie were the ones making everything really work.

And he'd certainly never take a bag of swag for granted again.

After an hour, he asked the kids if they were hungry. His question was met with a unanimous yes, and he ordered Chinese food from his favorite restaurant. It arrived just as they were finishing the last bag.

Julie brought out plates and napkins, and they sat around the conference room for another thirty minutes sharing food and joking around with each other.

At nine, a driver arrived to take the kids home, and he was finally alone with Julie.

She sat in the chair next to his and swiveled it around to face him. "You did good, Matt."

"I just followed orders. Maya is a manager in the making."

"She can be a little bossy, but she's good at taking charge. The other kids complain, but they usually look to her for her opinion, except for Hannah. They often seem to have a power struggle going on. Maya has the brains and Hannah has the looks, but they need to figure out how to use all of themselves and not just the one thing they know is true."

"That's a good point," he said, impressed with her insight. "They like you, Julie. You treat them with respect."

"I try. They don't always get respect in their personal living situations. Some of them are in foster care. Others are growing up with single parents. They all need to feel like they have a place in the world, and the program at Baycrest gives them that. Thanks to you and your participation in the cook-off, it's a program we'll be able to keep going for a while."

"I want to make a donation, too," he said. "Tell me what you need."

"You don't have to do that. I didn't bring you here to ask for money."

"I know. You brought me here so that I'd have to work to spend time with you," he said with a grin. "But I liked the kids and I liked what I heard about Baycrest, so we're going to talk about a donation—later."

She stiffened a little at his words and a nervous gleam flickered through her eyes. "Why wait until later?"

"Because I have something else I want to talk about now." He rolled his chair forward so his knees were touching hers, and then he leaned forward. "First, I have to kiss you, because it's been way too long." He pressed his lips to hers, feeling a surge of desire at the taste of her mouth.

He wanted to do a lot more than kiss her, but Julie spooked easily, and he forced himself to leave it at just a kiss.

Her eyes were burning bright when he met her gaze.

"I don't know what I'm going to do about you," she murmured. "I feel like I'm playing with fire."

"There are certainly a lot of sparks between us," he agreed. "I have an idea."

"Am I going to like it?"

"I hope so. I want to take you out tomorrow night. No dinner with friends—yours or mine, no work, just you and me."

"I'm so busy. The cook-off is Saturday night."

"You can't get away for a couple of hours? You just put in a twelve-hour workday, didn't you?"

"True, but that's the way this job goes."

"Come on, Julie. Meet me halfway."

"I've met you more than halfway, Matt. I don't know why you keep trying so hard. You could get any woman you want to go out with you tomorrow."

"But I want you." As he said the words, he realized just how true they were. What had started out as a challenge had turned into something that was a lot deeper and way more complicated than he'd ever imagined.

Julie stared back at him. "You don't quit, do you?"

He smiled. "I wouldn't be much of a ballplayer if I let a bad at bat keep me from trying again. You know that baseball is more about failure than success. A good .300 average means you're getting out 70% of the time. So, no, I don't quit, not when I really want to succeed. So what do you say?"

"Okay, I'll go out with you tomorrow night."

"Good." He was about to kiss her again when he heard a man's voice down the hall.

"That's my boss," Julie said as she got to her feet.

Matt rose as a middle-aged man with dark graying hair walked into the conference room. Surprise flashed in his eyes when he saw Matt.

"Matt Kingsley?" he asked.

"Yes."

"Robert Hudson."

He shook hands with Robert. "You're doing some amazing work here."

"Thank you. I must admit I did not expect to see you here. I hope there isn't a problem with your participation in the cook-off."

"Nope, I'm all set."

"Matt helped stuff the swag bags," Julie interjected.

Robert raised an eyebrow at that piece of information. "You asked him to do that?"

"I volunteered," Matt put in. "It was fun. I enjoyed meeting the volunteers."

"Well, thank you again," Robert said, obviously a little confused by everything. He turned to Julie. "I just stopped in to see if you needed anything."

"We're all done. We were just about to close up," she replied.

"Can I have a word before you go?" Robert asked.

"Of course. I'll just walk Matt out and then I'll be right with you."

"Thanks again for your help, Mr. Kingsley," Robert said.

"No problem." He followed Julie out to the front door. "I guess it was a good thing your boss didn't walk in a few minutes earlier."

Her cheeks turned pink. "That would have been embarrassing and unprofessional."

"So, tomorrow…will six-thirty work?"

She nodded. "I should be able to get away by then. Where are we going? What should I wear?"

"Whatever you want. You'd look beautiful in anything."

She shook her head and gave him a smile. "You do have a way with words, but that's not a very practical answer."

"Okay, then how's this? Wear something sexy."

"In that case, I might have to go shopping."

He laughed and gave her a quick kiss. "I'll see you tomorrow."

"You know, seeing each other this often means you're going to get sick of me pretty soon," she said lightly.

"That's a risk I'm willing to take."

Chapter Eleven

Julie dashed home after work on Friday, managing to get out of the office a little after five, which was quite the feat considering the cook-off was the next day. All afternoon, she'd thought about cancelling on Matt, but in the end she couldn't do that. Not just because she'd said she would go, but also because she wanted to go. She wanted to spend time with him, and even though she knew she was getting way too attached, she didn't care. She'd told herself it would all be over in a week when he left for spring training. So it wasn't like she had to end things now. They were going to end on their own in a few days anyway.

She spent the next half hour trying on outfits and discarding them just as quickly, Matt's request to wear something sexy ringing through her head. In the end, she settled on a short clingy black dress and heels that should work for just about anything. She brushed out her hair, leaving it long, applied a little makeup and tried to calm her nerves.

She'd spent a lot of time with Matt already. There was no reason to get worked up now.

Ending her nervous pacing, she sat down on her couch only to have her gaze fall on the envelope her mom had given her earlier in the week. She really should put it away, but for some reason she hadn't been able to touch it since she'd set it down.

Well, she certainly wasn't going to open it now. Tonight was about the present, not about the past.

A moment later her buzzer rang, and she jumped to her feet. At Matt's sexy "hello", she told him she'd be right down and then headed out the door.

He was waiting at her front door dressed in gray slacks and a button-down shirt under a black sports coat. He looked so good her mouth watered.

"Hello, beautiful," he said as she came through the door.

"Hi, Matt," she said with a smile. "You look good. I guess we clean up pretty well."

"That we do."

He took her hand as they walked out to the sidewalk, and she liked the way he wrapped his fingers around hers in a gesture that was both possessive and protective. Instead of Matt's sports car, she was surprised to see a black limousine double parked in front of her building and even more surprised when Matt headed straight for it. "What's this?"

"I hired us a car," he said, opening the door for her. "That way I can you all my attention."

He was definitely putting on the charm tonight, and she couldn't help but respond to it. There hadn't been anyone else who made her feel so special.

"Fancy," she said lightly as she got into the back, sliding along the luxurious bench seat to give Matt room to sit next to her.

A moment later, the car pulled away from the curb.

Matt reached for the bottle of champagne that was chilling in a nearby ice bucket. "Champagne?"

"You're pulling out all the stops."

He grinned. "Just trying to show you a good time."

"Then I'll have some champagne."

Matt poured them both a glass, then made a toast. "To tonight, to the beginning."

"The beginning of what?"

His eyes sparkled. "That's what we're going to find out, Julie."

She took a sip of champagne and the bubbles made her feel giddy. She needed to get a grip. She was a grown woman going on a date, not Cinderella on her way to the ball with a handsome prince, although it felt a little like that.

She cleared her throat. "You've really gone to a lot of trouble, Matt. You didn't have to. I'd have been happy with a cheeseburger."

"I know, which is exactly why I want you to have more. I've been thinking a lot about my life the past few days. Before I met you, being famous never bothered me. The women I've dated in the past have been thrilled to be part of the spotlight. But you're different. You don't want to be the center of attention, and you don't really want a man who is, either. I can't change who I am, or how people react to me, or the fact that nine times out of ten a fan will interrupt any date I'm on. But there is a flip side."

"There is?" she asked doubtfully.

"Yes. And I'm going to show it to you. I want you to forget about the past and not worry about the future. Let's just have tonight. What do you think?"

"I can't think of anything I'd rather do," she said, his words wrapping around her like a warm blanket.

"Then sit back and relax."

She sipped her champagne as the limo moved swiftly through the city. Dusk had settled over the city and the sky was a beautiful dark purple. A few minutes later, they crossed over the Golden Gate Bridge and drove through the hilly streets of Sausalito, finally stopping at the harbor.

Matt took her empty glass and helped her out of the car.

Then he led her down a pier and onto an enormously large and luxurious yacht. An older man in uniform welcomed them aboard.

"Captain Donovan," Matt said, shaking the man's hand. "This is Julie Michaels."

"Hello," he said. "It's a pleasure to have you both aboard."

"Thank you," she replied.

"Is everything ready?" Matt asked.

Captain Donovan nodded. "Yes, sir. Please go inside, make yourselves comfortable. We'll be leaving in a few moments."

"Great." Matt took her hand, and they walked down the stairs into a large, lovely salon. She had never been on a yacht before and was astonished by the spaciousness of the room. There were two long couches set under several portholes, and in one corner of the room there was an intimate table for two complete with silverware and flowers. The entire room was lighted with candles and there was a soft background of music.

"Wow," she said. "This is amazing."

"I'm glad you like it."

"I have to say I'm very impressed. You're batting .1000 so far."

"I'll try to keep it up," he said with a grin. "We'll eat in a little while. But in the meantime, why don't we go up on the deck and enjoy the cruise?"

"That sounds good to me."

They walked back up the stairs and over to the rail. Within minutes, the yacht moved effortlessly into the San Francisco Bay. The moon had risen and the stars were making their appearance in a bright, clear sky. The lights of the city and the bridge added to the incredible landscape. "It all looks so magical from here," she murmured. "You can only see the pretty parts."

"Have you ever sailed on the bay before?"

"Once but that was in the daytime. I've never seen this view at night. It feels a little spooky, heading towards the dark ocean though."

"Don't worry. We're not going far."

"I'm not worried," she said, giving him a happy smile.

He smiled back at her. "Good, because I would never let anything happen to you."

She knew he meant every word. Matt was the kind of man who took care of people. He was a protector by nature. She'd seen that when he was with his brother and also with his friends. And she was seeing it now, too.

Matt moved behind her, placed his arms around her waist and pulled her back against his chest as they watched the city go by.

"I can't believe I finally have you alone," he said.

"Isn't there a crew?"

"They'll stay out of the way. I thought about taking you to a really exclusive restaurant, but it seemed too public. I was afraid someone would want to take a picture or ask for an autograph, and I didn't want us to be interrupted. I wanted to have time with you that was both extraordinary and also private."

"This was a good choice." She was touched that he'd spent time thinking about the perfect date. "Is the yacht yours?"

"No. It belongs to a friend of mine."

"A rich friend."

"Yes, he does very well," Matt agreed.

His arms tightened around her waist, and she leaned back against him, reveling in the warm strength of his arms and the solid chest supporting her. When he lowered his head, his lips touched the corner of her ear and the brief caress sent another tingle through her nerves.

"Matt," she said, turning around in his arms.

"Yes?"

"Kiss me."

His eyes turned jade at her request. He brushed her mouth lightly, teasingly, before settling in for a long, deep kiss. The tension that had been building between them flared like a match to dry tinder. There was no slow buildup of passion but rather an explosive blast of heat.

Julie slipped her hands under his coat and pushed her body provocatively against his, enjoying the press of her breasts against his muscular chest, and the feel of his long lean legs intermingling with hers. She loved his taste, his touch, his smell—everything about him, and she wanted to get a lot closer than they were.

The yacht suddenly bounced over some bigger waves, and she stumbled.

Matt wrapped his arms around her and murmured in her ear. "It's getting a little wild out here."

"In more ways than one," she said with a helpless laugh.

"Maybe we should go inside," Matt suggested. "It's getting cold."

"Good idea."

When they entered the salon, a waiter greeted them and told them dinner was ready. He seated Julie and asked if she would like wine or a cocktail. Julie decided to stick with champagne while Matt ordered a beer.

After getting their drinks, the waiter served them a chilled seafood salad that looked absolutely amazing. It was the beginning of the most delicious meal she had ever consumed with steak, lobster, vegetables, potatoes and an exquisite dessert made up of chocolate and raspberries.

During dinner, they talked about San Francisco, movies, the last book they'd read, friends and family. With Matt, it was always a give and take. He didn't try to dominate the conversation and he was interested in her life. She liked that a lot.

After dinner, they went back out to the deck. Matt draped his jacket around her for warmth, and she loved the feel of his coat around her almost as much as she loved the way his arm hugged her against his waist. The bay was quieter now, the waves less restless, and the yacht made its way gracefully through the water.

Standing under the moon and the stars, Julie felt the tension begin to build once again, and by mutual accord, they turned into each other's arms.

She took the lead this time, her need driving her to start the kiss, to slide her tongue into his mouth, to take whatever she could get. She tilted her head, seeking to get closer, and Matt did the same. It just wasn't enough…

Her fingers flew down the front of his shirt, unbuttoning and pulling the material out of his pants. She wanted to touch him more intimately, and she sighed with satisfaction when her fingers found bare skin. His abs stiffened beneath her caress, and she reveled for a moment in her own power.

Then Matt pulled the shoulder of her dress down, his fingers slipping inside to cup her breasts. Her breath caught in her chest as he kissed the side of her neck, sliding his tongue along her collarbone and down to the swell of her breasts. He was driving her crazy.

"Matt," she whispered.

He lifted his head and gave her a long look. "Do you want to go inside, Julie?"

Yes, yes, yes…her tingling nerves replied, but while her body was ready for more, her brain was a little more cautious. Her heart was beating fast, too fast. She felt as if she were standing on the edge of cliff. She wanted to jump but she was suddenly paralyzed. What the hell was wrong with her? She wanted him. He wanted her. It should be so simple.

"Julie?"

"I do want to, but..." But what was the end of that sentence?

The air crackled between them at her hesitation.

Why couldn't she just say yes? Why couldn't she just leap without looking? Why couldn't she stop being so afraid to take a chance?

After a long moment, Matt pulled her dress back into place and stepped back. "It's fine, Julie. I get it."

She wasn't sure he did get it. "I'm sorry. I do want to be with you. Everything is happening really fast."

"You don't have to explain," he said, his words calm, but a dozen emotions running through his eyes. "I'll tell the captain we're ready to go back."

He disappeared so quickly she didn't have time to stop him. Not that she probably would have stopped him. She needed a minute alone to catch her breath.

She let out a long sigh. Was she being stupid? Being with Matt would probably be wonderful and amazing, and her body was literally humming just from kissing him.

But what about afterward? What about tomorrow? Or next week? Or next month?

If she slept with him, it was going to hurt even more when he left.

Another sigh passed through her lips as reality hit her in the face. Even if she didn't sleep with him, it was going to hurt when he left. She should never have let things get this far. But she had, and now she had to deal with it.

* * *

Julie woke up Saturday morning with a pounding headache and a fierce desire to kick something—maybe herself. After Matt's decision to abruptly end their cruise, they hadn't spoken much. Every time she tried to say something, he cut her off, telling her it was all fine. But clearly everything wasn't fine.

Matt had walked her to her door to say goodnight, but there'd been a distance in his eyes when he kissed her—a kiss that had chilled her to the bone, because it hadn't felt like goodnight but rather goodbye.

She told herself she should be happy that he was backing away. Wasn't that what she'd wanted? He'd obviously realized she wasn't going to jump into bed with him, and he'd decided she wasn't worth the trouble. All that stuff about liking her and wanting them to get to know each other had probably just been part of his play to get her to sleep with him. But he'd lost and she'd won.

Unfortunately, it didn't feel like much of a victory.

As she got dressed, all she could think about was the fact that she was going to have to see him again tonight at the cook-off. Not just see him, either, she was going to have to take care of him, make sure he spoke to the press, make sure everything was set up in his kitchen, help him if he had problems.

It was going to be a long evening if they weren't speaking to each other.

Her phone rang, and her pulse leapt into her throat, until she realized it was her mother on the line. "Hi," she said a little shortly.

"Did I wake you?" her mom asked.

"No, I'm actually getting ready to head out. The cook-off is tonight, and I have a million things to do before then."

"I won't keep you. I haven't heard from you since our rather intense conversation last Monday, and I've been worried. Are you all right, Julie?"

She wasn't all right, but her emotions had nothing to do with her mom's confession or her father's unopened letters. "I'm fine. I haven't looked in the envelope if that's why you're calling."

"You should do it when it feels right. I just wanted to make sure you and I were okay."

"We are," she said decisively. Whatever her mother had done, she'd done it out of love and to protect her child. Julie wasn't going to fault her for that. "We'll talk soon, okay?"

"Okay. Good luck tonight."

"Thanks." She'd no sooner ended the call when her phone rang again. This time her pulse had a reason to jump. "Matt?"

"Hi Julie," he said quietly. "Listen, I know you're busy getting ready for tonight, but I wanted to apologize."

"I thought we weren't doing apologies."

"Yeah, I know, but I don't want you to think that I was expecting anything last night. I got caught up in the moment."

"So did I," she admitted. "I'm just more cautious than you are, or maybe I feel like I have more to lose."

"That might be how you feel, but I don't know that it's true."

She gripped the phone more tightly, wanting to believe his emotions were as involved as hers were.

"Anyway," he continued. "We can talk about it later. I'll see you tonight."

"See you then."

She sank down on the couch and stared at the wall for a good minute, not sure how to feel about Matt's call. At least, he'd broken the tension between them, but what happened now or what happened next? She'd thought they were done—but maybe not.

Chapter Twelve

It was half past five when Julie took one last look at the grand ballroom of the Ambassador Hotel. The tables were set with glittering silver, the centerpieces were stunningly beautiful, and the exquisitely decorated celebrity kitchens ran along the walls, each space designed to represent each celebrity chef. She'd seen Matt come in a little while ago, but she'd been too busy running around to do anything more than wave.

Melanie came over to her. "It looks amazing, Julie. You did a great job."

"*We* did a great job, but no more congratulating ourselves until the night is over. I don't want to jinx us."

"I saw Matt Kingsley a few minutes ago. He asked where you were. I said you were running around like a mad woman."

"I have been doing that, but I think everything is set now. I was just about to head over to his kitchen to see if he needs anything."

"There's something going on between you two, isn't there?" Melanie asked, a curious look in her eyes.

She hadn't had time to fill Melanie in. Actually, that wasn't completely true. She just hadn't wanted to talk about her relationship—or whatever it was—until she knew exactly what was going on. "There is something," she admitted. "And I want to talk to you, but not tonight."

"Okay, but I'm going to hold you to that chat. And it's going to be soon."

"It's a deal." Julie left Melanie and headed across the ballroom.

Matt was standing in his kitchen. It had been decorated in Cougar colors with a baseball-themed décor. He'd donned the chef's hat they'd provided for him, but he hadn't started setting up his station yet. Instead, he was reading something on his phone with a perplexed look on his face.

"Something wrong?" she asked as she walked into his space.

"I can't find the recipe. I thought I put it on my phone."

"It's taped inside the cupboard," she said, opening the nearby door. "See."

"You think of everything," he said with relief.

"Part of the job," she said, thinking how good he looked in his black slacks and gray shirt, a dark blue tie around his neck. His green eyes were sparkling, and his brown hair had been tamed by some kind of product. He smelled enticing, as usual. She had it bad—really bad.

While she was looking at him, he was looking back at her, and there was a gleam of appreciation in his eyes. "You look incredibly hot tonight—the lady in red."

Her short red cocktail dress was a little sexier than what she normally wore, but Melanie had convinced her to buy it a few weeks ago, and she'd really had nothing else in her closet that would fit the event.

"Thanks," she said. "I figured a bright color would make it easier for the volunteers to find me."

"You would stand out no matter what you're wearing. You're a beautiful woman, Julie."

Her cheeks warmed at his words.

"I'd really like to kiss you right now," he added.

Her skin grew even warmer. "Matt. Don't say stuff like that." She took a quick look around, but there was no one nearby. "I really thought after the way things ended last night we were done."

"We're not done," he said seriously.

"We should be. This relationship has nowhere to go."

"I don't agree."

"You're really stubborn."

"So are you," he returned. "Something we have in common. I'm sorry things got awkward last night. You rattled me."

"I did?" she asked in surprise.

He gave her a solemn nod. "Big time, and I don't get rattled easily."

She licked her lips. "You made me dizzy."

A smile spread across his lips. "I like you dizzy. I like you every which way. I didn't mean to pressure you last night."

"You didn't. Honestly, I felt like all the pressure was coming from me. I—I haven't felt so out of control with anyone in a really long time—maybe ever. And you know I'm kind of a control freak, so that feeling is a little terrifying."

"I know exactly what you mean."

She drew in a deep breath. "Anyway, we can't talk about this now. The guests are starting to arrive as well as the press. And you need to start cooking."

"Then we'll talk later, after the event."

"Fine. You should put on your apron. We promised our sponsors the chefs would wear them while they were cooking."

"I'll put it on. Right now, I'm more concerned with cooking this meal I've volunteered to make and not burning the hotel down."

"You'll do okay."

"You keep saying that, and while I appreciate the pep talk, I can't help feeling very alone at this moment."

"You're used to performing in front of a crowd."

"Yeah, but that's when I know what I'm doing, when I've practiced more than once."

"Well, I didn't stop you from practicing." She paused. "But, just like I had the recipe waiting for you, I've also made sure you have a little more backup."

"What does that mean?" he asked with a hopeful look in his eyes.

"I got you a sous chef. To keep the contest fair, I asked all the kids from Baycrest to help out in the kitchens, but you have the most knowledgeable kid I could find." She waved her hand toward the young girl walking toward them. "Maya is a very good cook. She's used to cooking for her siblings, and she's going to help you."

"Hi Matt," Maya said.

"Maya. You're a lifesaver," he said, giving her a big smile.

"You're making a really easy meal; it won't be hard," Maya told him. "Don't worry. I'll tell you what to do. First thing, you need to do is to get organized." She headed over to the refrigerator. "Let's see what you've got."

"I'm going to leave you to it," Julie told him.

He grabbed her arm, his warm fingers sending the oh-so-familiar butterflies dancing through her stomach. "Thanks, Julie."

"Good luck. There's still a chance you could win, you know."

"I'm just hoping I don't poison anyone."

"Maya won't let that happen," she said, smiling as Maya started to bark orders at Matt. He was going to have his hands full with Maya.

Matt grinned. "She's going to kick my ass."

"Matt, are you listening?" Maya asked, waving her hand in the air.

"Sorry," he said, giving Julie's arm another squeeze before he let her go. "See you later."

"Later," she echoed, then headed back to the front of the ballroom. She was almost to the entrance when she ran into her friends. Liz and Michael, Andrea and Alex had come as well as Kate and Isabella. After going through a line of hugs and greetings, she took them over to their table.

"I put you guys near the judging table, so you'll have a good view," she said, as they all sat down. "I think the food is going to be amazing, too."

"Where's Matt?" Liz asked.

"He's in his kitchen getting ready to cook."

"I think I'll say hello," Alex said.

"I'll go with you," Michael added.

As the two men left the table, Julie was immediately besieged by questions.

"What is going on with you and Matt?" Kate asked.

"Are you guys dating?" Isabella wanted to know.

"Is it getting serious?" Liz wondered.

"Stop," she said, sitting down for a moment in the seat Alex had just vacated. "We've gone out a couple of times, and I like him, but you all know how I feel about baseball players."

"And he hasn't changed your mind yet?" Liz asked.

"Well, maybe a little," she conceded. "Actually a lot. He's really great," she said with a sigh.

Andrea gave her a knowing look. "I recognize that expression. You're falling for him. You have the same look Liz did when she reunited with Michael."

"And the same look you had when you got together with

Alex," Kate put in.

"Matt seems really nice," Isabella added. "And he liked you enough to come to my hip-hop class, which not all men will do."

"He's been doing everything right," she admitted. "But I just don't see how it could work. Even though I know he's not my father, he's still on the road several months a year, and he's surrounded by women. He also told me he doesn't think he wants kids. That would be a deal-breaker. It's better if I cut things off now, before they get started."

Liz laughed. "Oh, Julie. You've already started. You're falling for him."

"Then someone catch me and point me in a different direction," she said with a sigh.

"I would try if you really wanted that," Liz said. "But I think you owe it to yourself to see what happens. If he really doesn't want kids, then that will be a big decision for you, but if that was just a theoretical comment he made in a conversation he's probably forgotten, then I don't think you can really use that to end things, at least not until you have that talk."

"He's leaving for spring training in a few days. We're not going to have time to talk about anything."

"A lot can happen in a few days," Andrea said. "You just have to be open to the possibilities."

"I'm not very good at that."

"You're getting better," Liz said with encouragement.

"Sometimes you just have to close your eyes and jump," Isabella put in. "Take the risk. It's only the way to find out what's on the other side."

She looked around the group of supportive female friends and felt amazingly loved. "You guys are wonderful. Thank you for coming, for listening to me, for kicking my ass when I need it."

"We're always good for that," Liz said.

"So are you going to talk to Matt?" Andrea asked.

"Later. Right now I have to focus on work." She stood up. "Get yourselves some drinks and have fun."

* * *

"You do not look like you are having fun," Michael told Matt, a sympathetic gleam in his eyes.

"I'm just trying to get through the next hour." He nodded to Alex. "Nice to see you again."

"I heard you were dating Andrea's friend Julie. That was a surprise. You know what you're getting into, don't you?"

He wasn't sure exactly what Alex meant by that. "You mean with Julie's past?"

"Actually, I was talking about the women. They are a formidable force of friends, and they vet every guy who comes close to their group."

"He's right," Michael agreed. "You screw Julie over, and you're going to have seven women on your case."

"I'm not planning to screw her over," he said.

"Matt, you have to flip the scallops," Maya interrupted.

"Sorry," he muttered, flipping the scallops as Maya went to the back of the kitchen to work on the side salad.

"Who's your boss?" Michael asked.

"One of the kids Julie works with. Maya is awesome. She's saving my ass right now."

"Come by when you're done and we'll buy you a drink," Alex promised.

"I'll take you up on that."

As Alex and Michael walked away, Gary and Connie walked into his kitchen.

"Are you surviving?" Connie asked with amusement.

"Barely. Thankfully, I have a good sous chef."

"I can see that," Connie said.

"You guys look good. How's the bun in the oven?"

"Behaving," Connie said, rubbing her abdomen with a protective, caressing gesture. "Only a little morning sickness. I'm hoping that's as bad as it gets."

"Are you coming to Arizona with Gary?"

"Wouldn't miss it. We're leaving tomorrow. I'm looking forward to sitting by the pool and soaking up some sun." Connie paused. "Is Julie coming down for any of the games?"

He shrugged. "Doubtful."

"Really? I'd make sure she had a good time. And I think you're going to miss her."

He knew he was going to miss her. Every second they were apart he missed her. He would love to have Julie come down for a weekend, but he didn't think that was in the cards. At this point, he wasn't even sure she'd go out with him again. He'd messed things up the night before. Things seemed better now, but he had no idea what was coming next.

Every time he thought he was getting somewhere with her, he ran into her guard wall and was bounced back on his ass. He was getting a little tired of that, but he didn't want to give up on her, because he still believed in his heart that she was important, that he needed to give their relationship a chance, that she might just be the one he'd been waiting for.

"Matt?" Connie questioned.

He realized he'd lost track of the conversation. "Sorry, I'm a little distracted."

Gary laughed. "By the cooking or by her?" He tipped his head to Julie who was talking to some nearby guests. "She looks hot tonight."

"Matt, don't let the scallops burn," Maya interrupted again. "You should really tell your friends to talk to you later."

He smiled at Gary and Connie. "You heard the boss. Beat it."

"Fine, come by our table when you're done," Connie said.

"Don't screw up," Gary added.

"I'm going to try not to." He waved them away and concentrated on getting his food together for the judges.

Finally, everything was done, plated and ready to be presented. He felt tired and hopeful that he and Maya might have just pulled it off. He turned to his helper. "Thanks, Maya. You were awesome."

"I know," she said with a smile. "It was fun."

"Are you staying for the party?"

"Julie got me and the other sous chefs a table," Maya replied.

"Listen I owe you. How would you like to take a bunch of your friends to a Cougars' game?"

Her face lit up. "That would be great."

"You can come early and I'll introduce you to some of the other players. Tell Julie how many tickets you need, and I'll make sure you get into one of the games in the first two weeks of the season. Okay?"

"Great," she said, giving him a high five as she left the kitchen.

He picked up his plate and headed to the judge's table. The judges were made up of five of the top chefs in the city plus the mayor. He didn't have a chance in hell of winning.

When it was his turn to present, he set down his dish as a series of flashbulbs went off in his face. The judges tasted his food. One of them mentioned that the scallops were cooked perfectly, and the other said she was pleasantly surprised. He was going to take their comments as a win.

As he left the table, he was met by one of Julie's

coworkers who led him through a series of interviews and photo ops with both television and print news media. It was another half hour before he was done.

Then he went looking for a drink.

Chapter Thirteen

Julie was kept too busy during the event to spend any time with Matt, but she'd seen him from afar and was pleased by not only the appearance of his contest dish, but also by the way he dealt with the media. He was patient, attentive and his smile charmed everyone he met. She couldn't have asked any more of him. He really was a generous man at heart. He cared about people—his family, his teammates, the kids from Baycrest—maybe even her.

But watching him work the room couldn't help but remind her of all the times she'd watched her father do the same thing. She'd been on the sidelines then, in the background, just as she was tonight. However, tonight was her choice, she reminded herself. She'd put this event together. She'd asked Matt to do exactly what he done, so she could hardly complain that he'd done it too well.

Frowning, she turned her focus back to the event. Dinner was over. The plates had been cleared, and the band had started to play. While some of the guests were dancing, others were starting to leave. She headed to the reception desk to make sure the volunteers were getting the swag bags out.

Twenty minutes later, Matt entered the lobby. His eyes lit up when he saw her, and she felt the familiar flutter of butterflies in her stomach.

"There you are," he said. "I've been looking for you. You owe me a dance, Julie."

"I'm working."

"The party is almost over."

"She can dance," Melanie said, giving Julie a pointed look. "You haven't had a break all night, and I can cover this."

"I don't think the boss would like to see me dancing."

"Robert is on the dance floor with his wife," Melanie returned. "Go, have some fun. You've worked really hard and so has Matt."

"She's right. I have worked hard," Matt said, holding out his hand with an expectant look. "I think you owe me at least a dance."

"Okay," she said. "One dance."

His fingers curled around hers, and as they made their way back into the ballroom, she was very aware of the curious looks they were getting. Matt didn't seem to care what anyone thought, and to be truthful, she was a little too tired to care.

When they got to the dance floor, the band started a slow song.

"Perfect," Matt said.

She silently agreed, because moving into Matt's arms felt perfect. She probably should have tried to keep some distance between them, because so many people were watching them, but the music tugged at her heart. When Matt's arms tightened around her waist, she didn't resist. Instead, she moved closer, until her head came just under his chin. She closed her eyes against his chest as his hand caressed her back.

One dance turned into another, and she couldn't find the will to pull away.

Eventually the choice was made for her when the band ended their set. The night was over.

She reluctantly stepped out of Matt's arms as the few dancers that were left on the floor applauded the band. After clapping for the musicians, she wrapped her arms around her waist, feeling chilled now that Matt wasn't holding her.

"Looks like we shut down the place," Matt murmured.

She glanced around, realizing there were only about a dozen people left in the entire ballroom. "I didn't realize it was so late. I better go see if Melanie needs any help."

"I'll wait for you to finish up, Julie. I want to talk to you."

"You should just go home, Matt. It could be a little while."

"I'll wait. Do what you have to do. Take your time. I'm not going anywhere without you."

She smiled at the irony of his words. He wasn't going anywhere tonight, but in a few days that would change. His life would be an endless circle of baseball games and road trips. He would be going a lot of places without her.

* * *

The bright lights of Matt's car stayed right behind her during her trip across town. It was comforting to know he was there, but she also felt tense about how to handle their situation. When she was away from him, every cold rational argument about their relationship played through her mind. But when they were together, she found herself wavering, fighting off an emotional desire to be with him, if only for a little while. She needed to make a decision, take a step in one direction or another; she just didn't know what choice to make. Every path seemed filled with possible problems. Life had been a lot easier before she'd met Matt.

The ride to her apartment passed too quickly, and she was no closer to a decision than she had been when she left. Matt found a parking space down the block and met her at the front door.

He followed her up the stairs without a word, and his quiet only increased her tension. They were heading toward something; she just wasn't sure what that something was.

She unlocked the door and turned the lights on. "Do you want a drink? I can make some coffee or tea."

"No, I just want to talk to you, Julie."

She didn't like the serious gleam in his eyes now. "About last night? Because I think we covered that."

"No, about tomorrow. I'm leaving for Arizona for spring training."

Her heart skipped a beat. "I thought you were here until Wednesday."

"I thought so, too, but my agent called earlier today, and he's set up some talks with a sponsor on Monday. He needs me to be there. It's a pretty big deal."

"Okay," she said slowly. "I guess that's great for you, right?"

"It's lucrative. But I'm not happy about having to leave tomorrow. I wanted to have more time with you."

"Tomorrow…Wednesday…there's not much difference," she said, feeling suddenly overwhelmingly depressed. She tried to blame her weariness on the event, on the long night, but she couldn't keep lying to herself. She didn't want Matt to leave—ever.

"Julie," he began, then stopped.

She waited and then impatiently asked, "What? What do you want to say?"

"I know the timing isn't good, but I care about you, Julie, and I don't want this to end."

"I don't even know what *this* is," she said, waving her

hand helplessly in the air. "We've been having fun, but we've both known from the beginning that *this*, whatever it is, can't go anywhere. We're too different. Watching you tonight, surrounded by the press and your fans, reminded me of who you are. Yes, you showed me the flip side of fame with a beautiful cruise on a luxury yacht. But the rest of your life would be hard on me."

"It's hard on me, too. Do you know what it feels like to stand in front of a camera or a group of reporters and have to answer questions regardless of how personal or provocative they might be? Everyone wants a piece of me. Do this, do that, smile for the camera, take a picture with my wife, kiss my baby. And you're no different, Julie. You used me for your fundraiser. I spent the night performing for your organization."

"And I'm grateful."

"I don't want your gratitude. I just want you to see me and not your father. I'm tired of being blamed for his sins."

She stared at him in shock. She'd never seen him so angry before. She wanted to defend herself, but how could she?

"I'll let you in on a little secret, Julie," he continued. "Before I met you, I always wondered if a woman was with me because of who I was or how much money I made. I was never really sure if they just wanted to date a baseball player or if they wanted to be with me. Have you ever had to worry about that?"

"No," she admitted.

"It's difficult to know who to trust or how much to reveal. A woman I went on one date with five years ago sold a fabricated story to a tabloid with a photo she'd taken of me in bed while I was asleep. How do you think that felt?"

"Like a terrible violation of your privacy. I'm sorry, Matt."

"I don't want you to apologize."

"Then what do you want?"

"I want you to say you'll give a relationship with me a chance."

"You're leaving tomorrow."

"I'm going to Arizona, not the moon. You could come down on a weekend. If not, I'll be back in six weeks. In the meantime we can talk and text."

"You'll be busy."

"Not every second. And when I come back to the city, I'll have more time."

"When you're traveling and playing at least five games a week? How much time could you have?"

"We can make it work, Julie. We just have to both want to do that." He met her gaze head on. "I guess that's really what it comes down to, doesn't it?"

"It would be so strange to come to your games, to sit in the stands with the family, with the wives. I've already done that whole routine. I don't think I could do it again."

"Julie, you need to be honest," he said forcefully.

"I am being honest," she protested. "I've always been up front with you."

"With me, yes, but what about yourself? From what I've seen and heard, you love the ballpark, and you love baseball. After your father left, you locked away the good memories with the bad, but that doesn't change the way you feel about the game." He paused. "You fixed the hitch in my swing. You can separate the past from the present, your father's action from the sport. I know you can do that. I think you're handing to those old feelings because they're safe and comfortable, but you've changed."

She had changed, and she was shocked he could read her so well. "Okay, even if that's true," she admitted. "There are a lot of other obstacles between us. My job is as important to me as yours is to you, so even if I want to watch you play, I won't always be able to. I won't go on the road with you. I won't put my life on hold to support yours."

"I wouldn't ask you to do that."

"Are you sure you wouldn't feel like I didn't care if I wasn't there?"

"I don't watch you work, Julie—well, except for tonight—so I wouldn't expect you to do the same. Sure, it would be great to have you there, especially for big games, but I don't see your job being a huge problem."

She hated that he was taking each of obstacle and smashing it into a million pieces, but she still had a big one left. "What about children? You said you didn't want any, Matt. You raised a family already. But I didn't. And I've wanted a family since mine broke apart, maybe not today or tomorrow, but definitely in the future. I cannot see myself without kids."

"We can talk about that, Julie."

"We're talking about it now."

"Then let me say my feelings are not set in stone. But all that can be worked out down the road. Right now I just want you to say you'll go out with me again." He gave her a warm smile. "That's not so hard, is it?"

She sighed. "I am a lot of work, aren't I?"

"Yeah, but I think you're worth it. I just don't want you to worry about everything this second."

"Asking me not to worry is like asking me not to breathe. And you worry, too. You worry about your game, your brothers and sisters and the choices they're making."

"That's true," he admitted. "I worry about the people I care about and that includes you. But I don't let the worry control my life. I don't shy away from something or someone because it's complicated or it's hard. The things worth having usually are hard. I think we could be great together. I've never told anyone that before, Julie. I'm willing to take a risk on us, but you have to be willing to take that risk, too. Can you do that?"

She really wanted to. "I like you, Matt, and I didn't expect to. Nor did I want to, because love can be painful."

"It can be painful. But you're not living if you're not getting hurt. And if you don't go for what you want, you'll never know if you can get it."

"I wish I was as brave as you are."

"You are brave and beautiful and amazing. I want you in my life."

"How can you be so sure?" she murmured.

"Because I know who I am, and I know who I want." He gave her a long look. "I'm going to go now. I want to see you again. I want to be with you. But you're up, Julie. I took my swings. It's your turn now."

* * *

On the plane to Arizona Sunday morning, Matt wondered if he shouldn't have tried to play a few more innings before handing Julie control of the game. But it was too late for second thoughts. The next move was hers. And he really hoped that move would include a call or a text or maybe even a surprise appearance at spring training.

Connie slipped into the vacant seat next to him. She and Gary were seated a few rows back.

She gave him a smile. "How's it going? I haven't had a chance to talk to you since the cook-off last night. You and Julie were burning up the dance floor when I left."

"I had a good time," he said. "You?"

"It was fun. I even enjoyed eating your scallops. Now that I know you can cook, I'm going to expect an invitation to your house for dinner."

"Deal. But I'm sure the hotel catering staff did a better job with the recipe than I did."

"So Gary told me not to ask, but I can't help myself, because you know I'm nosy and I really care about you. What's going on with you and Julie?"

He let out a sigh. "I don't know."

"You're falling for her, aren't you?"

He had the terrible feeling he'd already fallen. "It's complicated."

"Because of her father?"

"That's part of it. She doesn't trust ballplayers."

"But you're more than a ballplayer; you're you," Connie returned. "Julie needs to find a way to separate you from what you do for a living."

"Believe me, I've tried to get her to do that. But she's got a huge wall up, and I've been butting my head against it since we met."

"It sounds like you're giving up," she slowly. "That surprises me. You don't quit, Matt."

"Not usually," he agreed. "But the season is starting, and we both know the time commitment that's involved. Maybe if I'd had a few more weeks to solidify things…" Even as he said the words, he knew that a few more weeks probably wouldn't have mattered. He'd tried to show Julie who he was, but if she couldn't see him now without the ghost of her father in the way, then she probably never would. That thought was discouraging.

"I like Julie. I think she's good for you, because she doesn't think you're a god like everyone else. She's also strong and independent and you need a woman like that. I've never known you not to go after what you want, Matt."

"I've been doing that, Connie, but now I'm on my way to Arizona—and she's not."

"Did you invite her to come down?"

"I did, but I don't think she'll come." He paused. "I think you and I are both going to have to accept that Julie is not going to be part of my life."

Connie frowned. "I don't want to accept that."

He gave her a frustrated smile. "Neither do I, but it's probably the truth."

* * *

Julie got up late on Sunday morning. After Matt left her apartment, it had taken her hours to fall asleep. Finally around dawn, she'd fallen into a restless slumber, waking back up around ten. Now, padding around her apartment in her PJs, she made coffee and flipped on the television. She watched the news for a while, then hit the remote repeatedly trying to find something to take her mind off of Matt. In frustration, she finally shut off the television and sat back with a sigh.

Matt had put the ball in her court. He'd told her he wanted to see where their relationship could go, and a part of her wanted the same thing. But she was looking further down the road than Matt was, and all she could see was disaster coming.

Was she being too cautious or paranoid? The answer to both questions was probably yes, but she'd spent the past ten years of her life trying not to get hurt, and it was all because of her father.

Her gaze drifted to the envelope on the coffee table.

What the hell was she waiting for?

Before she could remind herself of how much her father had hurt her, she grabbed the envelope and ripped it open. A stack of dozen or more letters had been banded together. She opened the first letter, which was dated February 24th, twelve days after her father had asked for a divorce.

She remembered that February so well. Her mom had been planning a Valentine's Day surprise, a trip to Maui for a week. She'd wanted to make it a second honeymoon. But two days before Valentine's Day, her father had come home really late. He and her mother had gotten into a horrible fight. She could still remember lying in her bed, staring at the ceiling and listening to the pain and anger in their voices. She'd heard her parents' door slam, and then her own door had opened.

She'd thought for sure it was her mom, but it was her dad.

He'd sat down on the edge of her bed, and said, "I'm sorry, honey, but things aren't going well with your mom and me. We've decided to get a divorce. I'm going to be leaving for a while, but I'll see you soon."

She had stared at him in shock. She'd had a million questions but she hadn't asked one. He'd kissed her on the forehead and left. It was the last real conversation they'd ever had.

Two sentences, she realized now, two lousy sentences.

He'd come by a week later, but she hadn't wanted to see him. By then she'd listened to her mom sob her heart out, and she was furious with her father for breaking her mom's heart and destroying their family. In dramatic sixteen-year-old fashion, she'd told him she hated him and never wanted to see him again.

Then he'd written her the infamous letter that she hadn't wanted to open, the letter that was now staring her in the face.

She slipped it out of the stack and finally slid her finger under the seal and pulled out a piece of notepaper.

With a deep breath, she started to read:

"I'm so sorry, Julie. I know I hurt you and your mom, and that you don't want to talk to me right now. That's okay.

You need time. I just want you to know that I love you very much. I'm divorcing your mother, but I'm not divorcing you. You're my daughter. That's never going to change."

Her eyes blurred with tears at words she'd always wanted to hear but never had.

Maybe because she hadn't allowed herself to hear them, she realized now.

She picked up the next letter, which was postmarked a month later. He'd obviously sent the note from the road.

"Julie, sweetheart, I miss you so much. I've tried calling a few times, but your mother says you don't want to talk to me and I should give you your space. Call me or write me. Just let me know you're okay. I know you may not believe me, but I worry about you."

She drew in a breath, her chest heaving with the weight of emotion as she wrestled with her feelings. On one hand, he had reached out to her with letters. On the other hand, she couldn't remember him ever showing up at the house or at school. Had he really tried that hard to see her?

The next letter surprised her with an answer. It was postmarked in May, three months after her dad left.

"I came by the house today and your mom wouldn't let me in. She's so angry about the divorce that she's doing everything she can to keep me away from you. I have a feeling you're probably not even getting my letters. I stopped by your school today. I thought I'd catch your softball game. Even if you didn't want to see me, I wanted to see you, but your coach told me you quit the game. I think it was then I realized how much you must hate me, because you loved to play. Apologies are never going to be enough, are they?"

An angry tear dripped down her cheek. Of course an apology wasn't enough. Saying he was sorry for ruining her life wouldn't change anything. It wouldn't make it all better.

But it was odd to think he'd gone to see her play softball.

She set down the letter and picked up the next one.

There was a two-year jump in time.

This letter included a photograph of a baby. Her heart came to a pounding stop as she stared at the one-week-old girl.

"I thought you might want to meet your sister, Amanda. She looks a lot like you as a baby. I want you to meet her one day. I hope with time you'll let me back into your life and that you'll be a part of Amanda's life as well."

She swallowed back a knot in her throat as she stared at the picture of her sister. Even though she'd known about her, she hadn't seemed like a real person.

How crazy that her father had started over with a new family in his forties, too. Was he a different parent now that he wasn't playing baseball all the time?

She set down the photograph as she suddenly realized that everyone had moved on but her. Her father had remarried and had more children. Her mother had remarried, too, and was happy with her new husband.

Was she the only person still stuck in the past?

Frowning, she knew there was only one answer—yes. The two people who had divorced had found love again, but she was alone. She was distrustful and wary and afraid to put her heart on the line. She had met a man who had made it clear he was interested in a relationship, and she'd done everything she could to push him away.

Not that there wasn't more between her and Matt than just her emotional baggage. There were other issues, too. But if she could open her heart up again, would all those issues become challenges instead of problems?

Matt was right. She did see the glass half-empty. Maybe she needed to see it half-full.

Stuffing the photos and letters back into the envelope, she decided she'd seen enough of the past for now. She had to start focusing on the present and the future.

Her doorbell rang, and she jumped to her feet in surprise. For a split second, she thought it might be Matt. Maybe he hadn't gotten on the plane after all.

But when she pushed the buzzer, it was Isabella's voice that rang out.

"Are you ready?" Isabella asked.

"Ready?" she asked in confusion.

"For brunch. Did you forget? I had a feeling you might with everything else that's been going on."

"I did forget."

"I'll wait for you. I'm double-parked, so get dressed fast."

"I don't know—"

"You're coming," Isabella said decisively. "We all want to hear what went on with Matt Kingsley last night." She paused. "Wait a second, is he with you? Did he stay over?"

"No, he didn't. I'm pretty sure it's over between us."

"Well come downstairs, and we'll help you figure it out," Isabella said.

She sighed. "All right." She might as well spend the day with her friends. At the very least brunch would take her mind off of Matt.

Chapter Fourteen

Brunch at the Cliff House in San Francisco was more fun than Julie had anticipated, and she was happy that her friend Maggie had made it down from Napa to join them. Maggie worked at a hotel and often had to miss out on weekend and evening events, so they didn't get to see her very often.

After they'd all caught Maggie up on their lives, the conversation turned to Julie's love life, as she'd figured it would. Since Liz, Kate, Andrea and Isabella had been at the cook-off, there was no point in denying that there was something going on with her and Matt Kingsley. But as she'd told Isabella earlier, she wasn't really sure if that *something* wasn't already over.

"Matt left this morning," she told them. "He had to go to Arizona sooner than he'd expected. He said he still wanted to have a relationship with me, but I can't see how that would work. I definitely didn't give him the answer he wanted. I'm pretty sure we're done."

"You can still talk to him," Liz said. "You have a phone."

"Or go see him," Isabella put in. "Arizona isn't that far away. You could be there in three hours."

"And then what? I sit in the stands and watch him play

baseball? I have a job. I can't run down to Arizona. We have our walkathon in three weeks. There's a ton to do before then. And after that we'll be gearing up for the telethon and then the summer events. My life is busy."

"You still have to take breaks for yourself," Andrea said.

"You're talking to me about taking breaks?" Julie asked with a pointed look.

Andrea acknowledged her point with a wry smile. "I know I work too much, and there have been days or years when I've been obsessed with my job. But after I met Alex, I realized that I needed more in my life than work. If I hadn't given him a chance to distract me, I would not be as happy as I am now. And we're working out the work-life-love balance. It's a constantly changing dynamic. You and Matt can do the same thing."

"Andrea is right," Liz said. "I've always taken my career seriously, but reuniting with Michael made me see how single-minded I'd been. Your career is important, Julie, but so is love."

Julie groaned, looking at Isabella and Maggie. "I need my still single friends to speak up now."

Isabella gave her an apologetic smile. "Sorry. Having seen you with Matt last night, I don't think it matters what I say. There's an attraction between you. Everyone could see that. So why fight it? Go with your emotions, with your heart. You have to feed your soul, Julie."

She could always count on Isabella, the free spirit in the group, to remind her of what was really important.

"What are you afraid of?" Maggie asked.

"Getting hurt. Losing myself. Loving a man I can't count on to be there when I need him," she said. "I don't want to be with someone whose job and life is so big that I can't be a priority."

"Of course you should be a priority," Andrea said. "If

you're not, then you should walk away."

"Right?" she said, glad to have someone finally support her position.

"But first you should find out if that's really true," Liz put in. "Because it seems like Matt has done everything he can to let you know he's interested in making you a priority."

"I agree," Maggie said.

"Me, too," Isabella put in. "You need to talk to Matt, see him again, maybe go on a few more dates before you end it forever."

"That shouldn't be too big of a hardship," Liz added. "He is a gorgeous, sexy, rich professional athlete."

She gave a helpless smile. "I'm crazy, aren't I?"

"You are," Liz agreed. "And I think you know that Matt is much more than what he does for a living."

She did know that. Matt had gone to a hip-hop class with her. He'd help her stuff swag bags. He'd made friends with a group of kids she loved. He'd put up with reporters and photographers to participate in her fundraiser. He'd taken her on a yacht cruise and tried to show her she was important to him.

So what was stopping her from taking the leap?

Matt had asked her what would it take for her to trust a man? She hadn't been able to give him an answer then. Could she now?

* * *

After brunch, Julie wrestled with indecision for a few more hours. She really wanted to talk to Matt, but in the end she realized there was someone else she needed to speak to first.

She called her mom. "Hi," she said. "I need a big favor."

"What's that, honey?"

"I need Dad's phone number. Is there any chance you have it?"

Silence met her request and then she heard her mother let out a harsh breath. "Are you sure?" Alicia asked.

"Yes. I read his letters, and I need to speak to him. He's been haunting me for too long. I don't think I can move forward until I get rid of the past, and he's the past."

"I have his number. He gave it to me a few years back, hoping that one day you'd want to reach out to him. I don't know if it's still good, but you can try."

She jotted down the number on her phone. "Thanks, Mom."

"Are you calling him now?"

"I think so, if I don't lose my nerve. Is it strange that I'm so nervous to talk to my own father?"

"No, but it's kind of sad," her mother said, a heavy note in her voice. "And I know that I'm to blame for a lot of the distance between you two."

"I don't blame you, Mom. I'm a grown woman and I have been for a while. The distance between us now is obviously on me."

"Will you let me know how it goes?"

"Yes," she said. "Talk to you soon."

She hung up the phone, took a deep breath and punched in the number her mother had given her. The phone rang once, twice, three times. Her gut twisted into knots. She was about to hang up, about to tell herself she'd tried and that was enough.

And then he answered.

The familiarity of his voice brought forth an overwhelming rush of emotion.

"Hello?" he said. "Hello?"

"Dad," she finally got out. "It's me—Julie."

"Julie?" he asked in amazement. "It's really you?"

Her hand tightened on the phone. "Yes."

"Are you all right? Is everything okay with you—with your mom?"

She was startled that he would even ask about her mother and that there was concern in his voice. "We're both fine," she said haltingly. "I just thought it was time to reach out to you. I finally had a chance to read through the letters you sent me over the years."

"I didn't think you'd ever read them."

"Well, I did." She didn't want to get into the fact that her mom had kept the letters from her until recently.

"Oh, Julie," he said. "There are so many things I want to say to you. And part of me just wants to hear you talk, because I haven't heard the sound of your voice in so long."

Tears gathered in her eyes, because she felt exactly the same way. "I know."

There was another long, tense pause between them. She knew they were both afraid to speak, to say the wrong thing, but so much time had passed already, she couldn't let any more time go by.

"I'm sorry," she said.

"You're apologizing to me?" he asked, shock in his voice. "No, that's not right. I hurt you so badly. I acted selfishly, Julie. I was so unhappy in my marriage that I made some big mistakes. I have a lot of regrets."

"I don't want to talk about the past anymore." She drew in a breath. "I was just thinking that maybe we could go from here."

"I would love to go from here. I want you to meet your sisters. I talk to them about you all the time. I've followed you from afar, Julie. Your grandparents have kept me in the loop. But you made it clear you didn't want me in your life, and I wanted to respect that."

"Well, I'm changing my stance on that," she said. "And I

would like to meet my sisters, but maybe not just yet. Maybe we just talk on the phone a few times before we all meet. I don't want to put them in the middle of any tension."

"I don't, either. We'll play it any way you want."

"Okay, then maybe we'll talk next Sunday."

"That long?"

"You know I'm not good with change," she said.

"Yeah, I know," he said softly. "Next Sunday it is. And Julie…"

"Yes."

"I've missed you."

"I've missed you, too, Dad." She ended the call with tears streaming down her face, but this time, they were happy tears.

* * *

Julie woke up early Monday morning, feeling energized and ready to take on her future. The phone call with her dad had definitely broken down her guard walls. She didn't know where that relationship would go, but she wasn't going to run from it anymore.

As for Matt, she still didn't know what would happen with him. There were a lot of things to work out, but she wanted to tell him about her dad. She picked up her phone and called him. It was only seven a.m., but she was hoping he was up.

"Julie?" he asked, his voice a little thick.

"I woke you up, didn't I?"

"No." He cleared his throat. "How are you?"

"I'm feeling pretty good actually."

"Really? I'm not sure how to feel about that, considering I'm here and you're there," he said dryly.

"That's not the part I'm feeling good about. I read my

dad's letters yesterday, and I ended up calling him on the phone."

"No way."

"Yes. I feel like I just got over a huge hurdle in my mind."

"Why did you decide to get in touch with him?"

"It occurred to me that both my mom and dad had moved on, and I was the only one stuck in the past. So I called him, and he was as shocked as you are. We didn't discuss too much, but we're going to talk again next weekend. We'll take things slow, see where they go."

"That's great, Julie. I'm happy for you."

"It's because of you, Matt. You made me realize I was holding on way too hard to the wrong emotions. I can't live my life with anger and bitterness. I wasn't hurting my dad; I was hurting myself."

"You were. And I'm glad you've made peace with him."

"Me, too." She paused. "You were the first person I wanted to call, Matt."

"I'm glad."

"I know I didn't give you the answer you wanted the other night, and maybe it's too late—"

"It's not too late," he interrupted.

"Okay," she said with relief.

"Damn, I wish I was in the city right now," he said. "I want to really talk to you, Julie, but I have to go in like three minutes and the rest of the day is packed."

"I understand. You're busy."

"And you're busy, too," he said. "I know you have a bunch of events coming up, and you can't come down here, and I can't leave, so can we take this relationship to calls and texts for a few weeks?"

"We can do that," she said, relieved that he wanted to keep things going.

"Good. Then I'll talk to you soon."

"Soon, she promised."

* * *

Three weeks later, Julie's relationship with her father was starting to feel a little more normal. They'd had three good phone calls and their conversations were staring to be more about the present than the past. Her relationship with Matt, however, felt far more frustrating.

With their very full schedules, it was difficult to find time to talk, and texting wasn't that great, but Julie kept telling herself to just hang on until spring training was over. Once Matt got back to San Francisco, they could have the real heart-to-heart they needed to have.

Fortunately, she had a lot of other things to concentrate on—like the walkathon.

The day of the walk, dawned with fog and a light rain, but when Julie arrived at the starting line on the Great Highway, there was still an air of excitement and determination, as if the bad weather was just another challenge to overcome. The walk would provide money for Children's Hospital, and many of the walkers had had kids who'd overcome terrible diseases or were still undergoing treatment, so no one was going to let a few sprinkles derail their fundraising efforts.

At eight o'clock, the mayor started the walk and nearly four-hundred walkers charged up the highway and along the route that would take them six miles through the windy, steep hills of San Francisco.

A mobile radio station cosponsoring the walk led the way for the first mile and then left to cover the walks going on in different counties. Throughout the morning Julie received reports and all signs pointed toward success.

Towards the middle of the race, she caught a ride with one of the police cars following the racers and was thrilled to see lots of fans along the route cheering on the racers.

And then an announcement came over the radio that made her heart stop.

Tragedy had struck.

The police officer turned on his siren as they raced across the city.

* * *

"I have to go to her," Matt said, charging into Dale's stadium office an hour before game time.

Dale stared at him in surprise. "What are you talking about? Who do you need to get to?"

"Julie. There's been an accident at her walkathon. I just heard it on the radio. I have to go to San Francisco now."

"Is she hurt?" Dale asked with alarm.

"It wasn't her. It was a kid, a teenager she works with. She's going to be devastated."

"Why don't you give her a call and—"

"I did call her and text her. She hasn't responded. I'm sure she's at the hospital. Look, Dale, you know I always put the team first, but not today, not this time."

"Okay," Dale said. "Go."

He was out of the office before Dale gave the okay. In reality, it wouldn't have mattered if Dale had said no, because he was going. Julie needed him, and he needed to be there for her.

* * *

When Matt arrived at the Emergency Room at San Francisco General Hospital a little after two, he found the waiting area filled with Foundation staff members, volunteers, walkathon participants and the media. He asked one of the news crew how the injured teenager was doing. She told him they were still waiting for him to get out of surgery.

It had been hours since the accident. Julie had to be going out of her mind with worry. He pushed his way through the room, ignoring the calls of recognition, intent on only one thing and that was getting to Julie, but she was nowhere to be seen.

He walked through the waiting room and into the corridor. Then he saw her standing against the wall, her arms wrapped around her waist as if she were freezing, her face pale, her eyes red and swollen from crying.

"Julie."

She started at the sound of her name. When she saw him, shock ran through her expression. Her mouth started to tremble. She bit down on her bottom lip and started to sway.

He jogged down the hallway and opened his arms to her.

She ran into his embrace, holding on to him as if she were drowning, and she'd suddenly found a life saver.

"I've got you," he said, wanting to give her as much comfort as he could. She felt ice cold, and her body was stiff with tension, but the longer they stayed together, the more she seemed to relax.

Finally, she lifted her head and gazed at him with teary eyes. "What are you doing here?"

"I heard about the accident on the radio. How is Ben?"

"He has a broken leg, maybe some internal injuries. I'm not sure. They took him into surgery hours ago. It's been so long. That can't be good."

"Just keep thinking positively. How did it happen?"

"They were just being kids, Matt. They were tired and cold; it was raining this morning. They thought they could take a shortcut rather than just admit they wanted to stop. We have vans all along the way, so that this kind of thing doesn't happen. One of the volunteers ran after them, but Ben dashed across a side street and a car came around the corner…" Her voice faltered and she drew in a quick breath. "This walk is to help kids, not to hurt them. I feel terrible. I asked the kids from Baycrest to walk. If anything happens to Ben…"

He put a finger against her parted lips. "Don't think about that right now."

"I can't think of anything else. Waiting is really hard."

"I know. I'll wait with you."

"I still can't believe you're actually here." She paused. "I've missed you so much."

His heart swelled with emotion. "I know. I feel the same way."

"Matt—I…" Julie paused, stiffening as a doctor came down the hall. "That's Ben's surgeon."

The physician stopped in front of them. "How is he?" Julie asked, slipping her hand into Matt's as they waited for the answer.

The doctor gave her a smile. "Ben is going to be fine. He has a broken leg, a couple of fractured ribs and a concussion."

"That doesn't sound like fine," Julie interrupted.

"It will take some time to recover, but he shouldn't suffer any lasting consequences."

"Thank God," Julie said.

"I'm going to let the press know," the doctor said, proceeding down the hall.

Julie blew out a relieved breath. "I am so relieved that Ben is going to be okay."

"Me, too. Do you want to get some air?"

"More than anything. I feel like I've been in this hospital for years."

They walked down the corridor and slipped out a side door, avoiding both the Foundation staff and the press.

"I can't believe it's sunny now," Julie said, lifting her face to the sky. "And warm. It feels good."

He couldn't help but agree, but while he wanted to give her a minute to catch her breath, he also wanted to get back to their earlier conversation. "Julie, you were saying something before the doctor came out of surgery, but you didn't finish."

She turned her gaze back to his. "Right. I was saying that I missed you. And now that my head is a little clearer, I also remember that you have a game today against Kansas City. How are you possibly here?"

"I told Dale I needed to be here for you."

"And he didn't care?"

"Well, I wouldn't go that far."

"Are you in trouble?"

"I'll deal with whatever comes. I've proved my loyalty to the team. Right now, I'm more interested in you. I want to tell you something, Julie, something I should have said before—"

"Wait," she interrupted. Me first."

"Okay," he said, not sure what she wanted to say, but he liked the sparkle in her eyes.

"I love you, Matt. I've been fighting it really hard. Because loving you is kind of terrifying. But you know what's even scarier? Not having you in my life. That's unacceptable, so whatever it takes for us to be together, I am up for it. I'm in—one hundred percent." She let out a breath. "Okay, now you."

"I love you, too, Julie." He smiled at the relief that flashed through her eyes and tucked her hair behind her ear in a tender gesture. "And that is scary as hell, because you're not an easy woman."

"That's what you love about me, right?" she teased.

"It is. But what I really love about you is your heart. It's huge. And I want all of it. I'm selfish that way."

"It's already yours, Matt."

"I know I'm not offering you the easiest of lives, but I'll do everything I can to make you happy."

"I want to make you happy, too. I would rather have a limited time with you than no time at all. You've changed my life, Matt. You've woken me up, and I am more than ready to give us a chance to be good together." She gave him an emotional but happy smile. "So what now?"

"We could go back to your place or my place or any place," he suggested, wanting to get her alone.

She groaned. "And I really, really want to, but I have to help the staff with the clean up and then there's the press and volunteers to deal with. I'm not trying to make an excuse or postpone anything, but—"

"But you have work to do, and you wouldn't be the woman I love if you didn't follow through on your commitments."

"You understand," she said, meeting his gaze.

"I do. I should get back to Arizona, too. I'll be home in three weeks for Opening Day."

"That seems like a good day for us to kick things off. I want to come and see you play, Matt. I want to be there for you."

"I like the sound of that, but I just found out your dad is going to be throwing out the first pitch on Opening Day. I know you're talking again, but are you ready to see him in person?"

"I am," she said without hesitation. "I'll tell him I'm going to be there. Maybe he'll bring his daughters, and I'll finally meet my sisters. I actually think it would be beautifully ironic for that to happen at Opening Day."

He tipped his head. "You've really come full circle, Julie."

"It's not a circle, because I didn't end up at the same place. And that's because of you."

"I'm glad I could help. One more thing," he said. "I know I told you I might not want kids, but honestly I was just frustrated with my siblings when I said that. I can't think of anything better than a little girl who looks just like you."

"Are you sure?"

"I'm sure about children and about you. I'm just not sure how I'm going to make it through the next few weeks without seeing you."

"Me, either. So give me a kiss that will last until Opening Day."

He smiled. "Now that's a challenge I can't resist." He wrapped his arms around her and showed her just how much he loved her.

Chapter Fifteen

Three Weeks Later

Opening day at the ballpark was blessed with brilliant sunshine, a warm breeze and the sparkling laughter of thousands of fans eager to embrace the beginning of a new baseball season. Julie, Liz and Isabella walked down the stairs to their reserved seats behind the Cougars' dugout. Julie felt nervous, excited, as if this day was the first day of the rest of her life. She and Matt had spoken every day since he'd gone back to Arizona, sometimes more than once, and every time they talked, she fell more in love with him.

But today would be the real test. She knew she couldn't just accept that Matt's life was in baseball, she had to embrace it. She didn't want his life to be separate from hers. Over the past month, she'd begun to realize that it wasn't just physical distance and time that had separated her parents but also emotional distance and an unwillingness to really try to love what the other person loved. She wouldn't make the same mistake.

"These are great seats," Liz said as they sat down in the second row.

"Only the best for the star hitter's girlfriend," Isabella teased.

She smiled at both of them. "Thanks for coming out with me. I'm not quite ready to sit with the wives and families yet. The only one I know is Connie, and she isn't coming, because she's been having some bad morning sickness."

"Don't worry. We're always here for you," Liz said.

As they sat down in their seats, Julie saw Matt walk out of the dugout. He looked into the stands, and when he saw her, a huge smile spread across his face. His eyes sparkled as he looked at her. They were a dozen feet apart, surrounded by thousands of fans, but in that moment it was just the two of them. She could see the desire and the promise in his eyes. He wanted to talk to her, but they'd both agreed they'd speak after the game.

Finally, Matt gave her a small wave and walked back into the dugout.

"That was intense," Liz said dryly. "I felt like I was watching the last scene of a movie where the hero and heroine finally find each other and admit their love."

"He just smiled at me," Julie said, knowing that Liz was right. A lot more had passed between them than a smile. Her stomach tightened as the players lined up on the field for the introductions and the ceremonial first pitch.

"Remember to breathe," Liz advised as Jack Michaels walked out to the mound.

"It's okay," she said. "We're good now. Or at least we're on the way to good."

Two adorable blonde girls wearing Cougars t-shirts and jeans accompanied her father to the mound. He held each of them by the hand, and they were clearly delighted to be with him and happy to be in front of a huge crowd. Her sisters, she thought with a wave of yearning. She wanted to get to know them. She couldn't believe now that she'd let so much time pass in anger and bitterness. But hopefully they could forge a relationship going forward.

The announcer introduced Jack with a long list of his accolades, and the fans went wild, the cheering getting louder with each accomplishment.

Julie couldn't believe the feeling of pride that swept through her. She hadn't been proud of her dad in—forever, but seeing him now, getting the acclaim he so loved, she couldn't help but acknowledge that he'd had a remarkable career. He'd lived his dream.

It was time to live hers.

Jack stepped up to the mound and rubbed the ball between his fingers. Then, like he'd done so many times before, he pulled back his arm and threw the ball to the plate. It was a dead-on strike with almost as much power as he'd had in his last game almost a decade earlier. The crowd broke into another round of applause.

Jack waved and picked up his youngest daughter with one arm and held on to the other one's hand as he walked back toward the Cougars' dugout. He spoke to the team for a few moments, and Julie felt another knot of emotion in her stomach when Matt and her father shook hands. She'd told her dad during their last phone call that she was in love with Matt, and he'd been shocked but pleased. He was probably hoping that Matt could help bring the two of them together, but she didn't need Matt to fix her family. She could do that for herself.

After leaving Matt, Jack walked up into the stands with the girls.

Julie stood up. Her father stopped in front of her, and she was shocked to see moisture in his eyes.

"Julie," he murmured. "You're beautiful."

She drew in a shaky breath. "Dad. It's good to finally see you again, too."

"I want you to meet Amanda and Grace." He paused,

looking at his girls. "This is Julie."

"You're our sister," Amanda said with a happy smile.

"I am," she admitted.

"They'd love to talk to spend time with you," her dad said. "When you're ready."

"You know what, Dad, I'm ready. Why don't we get together this weekend?"

He looked surprised but pleased. "This weekend is perfect."

She said goodbye to the girls and then sat down, relieved to have the last hurdle behind her. It had been one thing to speak to her dad on the phone and another to see him face-to-face.

"You okay?" Liz asked with concern.

"I'm great. Now all I need is for Matt to have a good game."

"I don't think you have to worry about that. He's one of the best."

"He is," Julie agreed, but she wasn't talking about baseball.

Nine innings later, Matt had hit a double and a triple, and the Cougars won the game by four. As the crowd left the stadium, Matt opened the field gate and walked up the stairs to say hello. She threw herself into his arms, giving him a hug and a kiss, without a single worry about who was watching.

"Good game," she said.

"I was trying to impress you," he replied with a smile.

"I've been impressed since I first met you," she replied.

"How was it seeing your dad again, hearing the crowd cheer for him?"

"Surprisingly good. I'm going to spend time with him and the girls this weekend. I'd like you to come."

"I will." He paused, giving her a long, loving look. "I'm

so happy to back in the city with you."

"Me, too," she murmured. "I love you, Matt."

"And I love you, Julie—more than I've ever loved anyone in my life," he said with complete and utter sincerity. "I'm going to spend the rest of my life making you as happy as I can."

"Me, too." She pressed her lips against his, sealing their promise with a kiss.

* * *

Isabella looked over at Liz with a dry smile. "Another single woman bites the dust. I'm beginning to think I'm going to be the last girl standing."

Liz laughed. "Love comes when you least expect it. I certainly never thought Julie would fall for a baseball player."

"They look happy," Isabella said, watching Julie and Matt kiss and laugh, then kiss some more. She wanted that for herself one day, but she couldn't quite imagine it happening. She hadn't met anyone who made her dizzy in a very long time.

"Looks like we'll be gearing up for another wedding," Liz said.

"Let's get through yours first. Did you finally decide on a venue?"

"The Stratton in Napa. Maggie is getting me a deal. We're going to tie the knot the second week in June. So mark your calendar."

"I've got it down," Isabella said.

"Hey, guys," Julie interrupted. "I'm going home with Matt."

"We figured," Isabella said, as she got to her feet.

"Let's all get together soon," Liz added as she stood up.

"We'll see you both soon," Matt promised. "But I need Julie to myself for a while."

Isabella smiled a little wistfully as Matt kissed Julie again. Love did look like a lot of fun. Maybe she should give it a whirl—one day.

THE END

Watch for Isabella's story—coming Spring 2015!

Book List

The Callaway Family Series
#1 On A Night Like This
#2 So This Is Love
#3 Falling For A Stranger
#4 Between Now And Forever
#5 All A Heart Needs
#6 That Summer Night
#7 When Shadows Fall

Nobody But You (A Callaway Wedding Novella)

The Wish Series
#1 A Secret Wish
#2 Just A Wish Away
#3 When Wishes Collide

Almost Home
All She Ever Wanted
Ask Mariah
Daniel's Gift
Don't Say A Word
Golden Lies
Just The Way You Are
Love Will Find A Way
One True Love
Ryan's Return
Some Kind of Wonderful
Summer Secrets
The Sweetest Thing

The Sanders Brothers Series
#1 Silent Run
#2 Silent Fall

The Deception Series
#1 Taken
#2 Played

About The Author

Barbara Freethy is a #1 New York Times Bestselling Author of 41 novels ranging from contemporary romance to romantic suspense and women's fiction. Traditionally published for many years, Barbara opened her own publishing company in 2011 and has since sold over 4.8 million ebooks! Nineteen of her titles have appeared on the New York Times and USA Today Bestseller Lists.

Known for her emotional and compelling stories of love, family, mystery and romance, Barbara enjoys writing about ordinary people caught up in extraordinary adventures. She is currently writing a connected family series, The Callaways, which includes: ON A NIGHT LIKE THIS (#1), SO THIS IS LOVE (#2), FALLING FOR A STRANGER (#3) BETWEEN NOW AND FOREVER (#4), ALL A HEART NEEDS (#5), THAT SUMMER NIGHT (#6) and WHEN SHADOWS FALL (#7). If you love series with romance, suspense and a little adventure, you'll love the Callaways.

Barbara also recently released the WISH SERIES, a series of books connected by the theme of wishes including: A SECRET WISH (#1), JUST A WISH AWAY (#2) and WHEN WISHES COLLIDE (#3).

Other popular standalone titles include: DON'T SAY A WORD, SILENT RUN, SILENT FALL, and RYAN'S RETURN.

Barbara's books have won numerous awards - she is a six-time finalist for the RITA for best contemporary romance from Romance Writers of America and a two-time winner for DANIEL'S GIFT and THE WAY BACK HOME.

Barbara has lived all over the state of California and currently resides in Northern California where she draws much of her inspiration from the beautiful bay area.

For a complete listing of books, as well as excerpts and contests, and to connect with Barbara:

Visit Barbara's Website:
www.barbarafreethy.com
Join Barbara on Facebook:
www.facebook.com/barbarafreethybooks
Follow Barbara on Twitter:
www.twitter.com/barbarafreethy

46824096R00104

Made in the USA
San Bernardino, CA
16 March 2017